The Legend Of Heath Angelo

By
N. Robert Winters

Author's Note

Although this novel is based on real people, the events and encounters are a work of historical fiction. I would like to thank Peter Steel, Heath and Marjorie Angelo's grandson, who is currently the manager of the Angelo Coast Range Reserve, for information about his family.

"Everybody needs beauty as well as bread, places to play in and pray in, where nature may heal and give strength to body and soul…" John Muir rwinters2350@yahoo.net

First Paperback Edition
Printed in the United States of America

ISBN: 1453646132

JUNE 12, 1977

The hummingbird stood still in the air looking at us before deciding that we did not pose a threat, then it quickly swooped in and grabbed cotton from a ball put out by my host, Heath Angelo.

"They take the cotton for their nests; much better than putting out sugar and water like some people do to attract them. They should eat nectar and help pollinate plants like Mother Nature planned. 'Birds and bees', you know."

We sat on Mr. Angelo's deck of his rustic cabin. From the front porch we could see Elder Creek flowing swiftly, run off from the winter rains. The meadow in front of the dwelling blazed with blue Lupin and yellow mustard in the late afternoon sun. Behind the creek towered trees of virgin Douglas fir forest, never logged. The smell of spring flowers mixed with the fragrance of the bay laurel leaves from the wet woodlands.

Heath poured me a shot of George Dickel Bourbon that he kept for guests to his remote abode. Visitors were few. Mr. Angelo lived in the middle of a seven thousand acre nature preserve with only a narrow dirt road meandering by his house. His gray hair and the lines in his face showed the years of love and loss that the old man had endured throughout his life. One of his loves surrounded us, it was his legacy.

"To the Northern California Coast Range Preserve. It's so good to be here." I said as I lifted my glass and toasted the gentleman.

"Do you want a cookie?" Mr. Angelo offered me one from a glass jar. "Sometimes my friends bring me cookies as a gift. When men bring me cookies, I put them in this jar with cookies brought by girls, and the cookies mate and make more cookies", he said with a twinkle in his eye.

"Thanks", I said and took one of the chocolate chips, not wanting to know its sexual orientation.

I came to the preserve to run a Youth Conservation Corp Camp for the summer, hired by the Nature Conservancy, an organization that buys land to preserve it. Mr. Angelo had deeded his land to the non-profit corporation and they had purchased adjacent forest to add to the acreage. The contract insured that Heath and two generations of his offspring could continue living at his family home. I had recently graduated from Sonoma State University and spent a year teaching before being hired to be the director of the camp. Sixteen teenagers would arrive the next week to work on the preserve and build trails on the other forest land. I was living in the campgrounds making ready for the teen arrivals to the Mendocino wilderness. I had backpacked and hiked for many years in the western mountains but I had never seen a spot more serene and beautiful than Mr. Angelo's front yard.

Mr. Angelo held up the bottle of bourbon and asked, "Do you want another?"

"Sure," I said, "I would like that."

Heath poured another shot of the amber liquid. This was my first of many visits to the benefactor's front porch.

"You wouldn't believe what happened to me this morning." I said. "I woke up to the sound of a crash in the kitchen and I jumped out of my sleeping bag and ran to see what was making the noise. A ring-tailed cat was standing there with his hand in the granola jar. He looked at me and I looked at him and I'm sure we both thought 'What the heck do we do now?' I went to get a broom and when I came back the animal was gone. All I can remember was his tail looking like the Cheshire cat in Alice in Wonderland."

Heath laughed. "I've seen ring-tails before but they're real shy, not like their cousins the raccoon. But the forty-niners called them miners' cats and even kept them as pets."

"I wonder if I'll ever see him again." I never did. As I was telling my story, two does came out of the woods to graze in the meadow. They had no fear of Heath, being totally protected from hunters like all animals in the preserve. "So, Bob, I hear you have a dog and you couldn't bring him to the preserve. Where is he?"

"Staying with a friend for the summer. I'll miss him."

"Maybe you can make a pet out of the ring-tail." He took a sip of whiskey and laughed.

"We have some time till I have to get back before sunset. I'd love to hear some stories about yourself and this preserve."

The elder gentleman looked at me for a long second, and then said "I can tell you a story or two. Maybe by the end of the summer we can exchange a few tales."

APRIL 18, 1906

It was still dark when the ground shook and Heath was thrown out of bed. The bricks of the fireplace and chimney of his house tumbled like they were wood toy blocks knocked down by the hands of the fifteen-year-old boy. His wood-framed Victorian two-story house rocked and rolled on its foundation, but stayed upright.

Heath hit his head hard on the floor. He was dizzy and nauseous like a seasick sailor on a ship for the first time. "What happened? Where am I? What day is it?" He stared up at the ceiling as the house rolled in an aftershock. The boy staggered to his feet and felt his way to flip the switch for the new electric light hanging over his bed. Nothing happened in the dark lonely room. He had no understanding that he was trapped in an event that would change California forever.

The boy found the doorknob and had to pull hard to open the door that slid open so easily only yesterday.

"Mom!" he yelled at the closed door of the room across the hallway at the top of the stairs.

"I'm here, son!" He heard her unsteady voice yell back.

He barged into her room and was greeted by the silhouette of his night-gowned mother as the first light of dawn filed through the curtain window at the other end of the room. They hugged, grabbed each other's hand tightly and walked unsteadily down the stairs, his mom holding firmly to the banister. They went out the front door.

Dawn was sending light to the small town of Alameda, located on an island jutting out from the east side of San Francisco Bay, just across the estuary in Oakland. Heath realized that he was dressed in a white cotton nightgown and the morning cold snapped him out of his daze. He smelled smoke and saw flames lick out from the roof of a house two blocks to the west. He heard the sound of the new fire truck with its bell clanging. Alameda had both a new fire truck and a horse drawn wagon at the turn of the century.

Finally his mom broke the silence "That was an earthquake wasn't it?"

"I think so. Are you as cold as I am?"

"Yes." She said but stood aimlessly.

Heath ran into the house, grabbed two throw blankets, came back and put one over the shoulders of his mother and pulled on the other like it was a big overcoat. He did not want to go back upstairs yet to get his clothes.

"Mom, do I have to go to school today?" The woman turned to her son, looked at him intently, and tears welled up in her eyes. She hugged the boy tightly, not wanting to let go. "No, I don't think you need to go to school today. I have a feeling there won't be school today."

Day was breaking, and as the light illuminated the street, Heath could see that people were gathered in the road, many with nightgowns or robes, a dazed look on their faces. Another aftershock hit and Heath threw himself to the ground, hoping to avoid falling. The young man heard more bricks falling and just then noticed the condition of the chimney on his house. Bricks were scattered on the south side of the dwelling and into the street. He noticed that many of his neighbors' brick houses had serious damage.

"Mom, look." Heath said and pointed to the bricks all over the street. The fire from the house two blocks down grew but he could see there were already streams of water being hosed onto the blaze. People were already starting to mobilize, piling bricks out of the middle of the street and in front of houses. "Mom, can I go help?"

The woman looked at him longingly but said "If you must, but I want you to check in with me by lunchtime."

The boy carefully ascended the stairs, threw on a pair of Levis, a flannel shirt, and grabbed a wool sweater. He hurried down the street to the closest fire, while noticing other fires on the island, most of which started when fireplaces had collapsed. Firemen, both volunteer and professional, would be spread thin.

"I'm here to help if you need me," he yelled to the fireman aiming water from a hose. The yellow rain coated man said to the boy, "Kid, grab the back of the hose behind me and keep it steady."

The flames were retreating from the timely attack of water. After about fifteen minutes, a volunteer with a fire helmet came over and relieved Heath on the hose. "I've got it from here." He said.

Heath was then free to wander around the village assessing the damage. He met up with Joe Silva, a friend from school. They noticed that most of the wood houses seemed to have just superficial damage except for the collapsed chimneys. Buildings made of brick were heavily damaged. As the boys were scouting the neighborhood, they noticed an overflowing ferry pulling into the dock. The boat stopped at Alameda on the way to Oakland from San Francisco. The 10:23 arrival was full of passengers carrying luggage, boxes, anything they could carry, leading the beginning of an exodus from earthquake damage in San Francisco to the east bay. Most of the passengers were going on to Oakland, but a few got off the boat at the Alameda mooring, and spread the news of the fire enveloping the city to the west. Hundreds of buildings were heavily damaged and multiple fires were blazing out of control all over the San Francisco Peninsula, whipped by the ocean wind.

The boys ran across the island to the beach on the bay and looked west. They could see the smoke rising from the city. Watercrafts of every type were on the bay. Those with motors mixed with masts leading an escape for a stunned and threatened populous.

By noon, the friends were back at Heath's house where Mrs. Angelo was running an assembly line, making salami sandwiches. Take one each boys, I'm making the rest for the neighbors whose houses were badly damaged."

"Mom, have you seen all the people coming across the bay from San Francisco? They say the city is a disaster and fires are burning everywhere. We were told that Marshall Law has been declared and the army is shooting looters. I hope dad is okay.

As they were eating at the kitchen table, a powerful aftershock rocked the house sending dishes and china knickknacks to the floor. Mrs. Angelo had just finished sweeping up all the glass from the morning spillage. The stress momentarily overwhelmed her and she sat at the table and cried. Heath got up, put his arms around her shoulders and kissed her on the cheek. He never saw her cry like this, even during the divorce.

"Do you want me to finish the sandwiches?" he asked.

His mother wiped her face in a dishtowel. "No, I'm alright. I'll finish the sandwiches, but I need you to sweep up. Then go out to the street and pile bricks from the chimney. It looks like I'm going to need your help all afternoon. We need to pitch the big camping tent in the backyard. People are going to need places to sleep."

As he finished his chores in the early afternoon, Heath could see smoke starting to hover over the bay mixing with the natural fog. He could smell it coming out of the west. Then he heard an explosion. The army in San Francisco had started using dynamite to build firebreaks. The military's well-intended but futile attack did almost as much damage as the earthquake. The seismic waves had damaged the water mains underground rendering the mostly modern fire department helpless.

Heath watched the setting sun explode in an orange glow in the smoky sky above the bay. Heath thought about his father in San Francisco wondering if he was all right. A chill grabbed him as wind whipped down his shirt. Heath never really worried about his father who seemed amazingly resourceful and self-sufficient, until he heard the first explosion. His dad had moved to San Francisco after the divorce two years ago. They did not see each other often but the man was still a big part of the boy's life. Now he yearned for his father like he did right after their first separation.

His parents had fought so much in the months before the divorce, what he remembered most about his father's absence was the quiet. His parents were no longer screaming at each other. His mother actually seemed relieved. Yet, as the evening closed in, he realized he missed his dad on this fateful day.

Then out of the glow coming from the dock he saw the familiar figure of his father. For the first time since he had been thrown out of bed that morning, he felt safe.

MAY 1, 1906

The ferry building stood above the smoky fog-laden ruins of the city, the flagpole on top was tilted to the south pointing to the direction of the epicenter, where the movement of continental plates caused so much destruction. As Heath approached the boat landing, he noticed the overwhelming smell of smoke blowing towards him. He was with his buddy, Joe, let loose from the steady stream of chores assigned by his mother since the earthquake.

The boy was happy to get out of the house which he felt was no longer his home. It was overrun by three new families. Mr. and Mrs. Antonelli of North Beach were living in what was formerly the office, the room next to his. When he was around they would speak in Italian so he couldn't understand what they were saying. It was so annoying. Before their exodus, they had run a successful import business.

Worse, the Lancings were planted in the living room, filling the first floor with four people including a brother and sister combination running around like little whirlwinds. Tim, at five, and Sarah, at four, were everywhere in the lower level of the house. Only blankets hung from the ceiling gave this family of four any privacy.

Outside living in the camping tent was another family, the Perkins, including their seventeen-year-old daughter, Lisa. Coming from Nobb Hill the girl thought she was a princess, way too good for the likes of a commoner like Heath.

Laundry was hung everywhere. While his mother did most of the cooking, he felt he was overwhelmed with work after school. The kids downstairs sent a constant torrent of noise up to his room when Heath tried to do homework. 'How did large families with lots of children manage?' He wondered.

The boys were going to visit Heath's father, Alfred, who was living at his business in North Beach. The senior Angelo did not want to move to the east bay because he had a business to run. In spite of the devastation, many enterprising people were already returning to work. Mr. Angelo's warehouse did not burn and his box and basket business was back in operation, though limited by a depleted work force. He knew people would need boxes to ship their surviving goods back east. He also knew he had to line up a supply of lumber because he would be in competition with contractors needing wood to rebuild the city.

The two young compadres had planned an exploration of the damaged metropolis so they were taking the long way to the warehouse. The boys started down Market Street with its broad avenue and grand brick buildings, wrecked and emptied. Soldiers could be seen everywhere, standing in pairs with little left to do except lean on their weapons. Instead of storefronts, people were selling their wares out of pushcarts and wagons. Crude handmade signs advertised goods and services. Capitalism quickly returned to the streets with everything for sale and all prices negotiable.

Heath and Joe turned north along Battery Street, the bar and red light district. They passed the federal custom house, its concrete walls scarred but intact, protecting the trade currency that would be needed to help refinance the rebuilding of the city. Two bars were open on the same block in a line of buildings that seemed untouched by the fire. A drunk staggered out of the saloon into the smoky sunshine at ten thirty in the morning. The famous Barbary Coast was still alive. The drunk was lucky he was not hit over the head and shanghaied on a ship bound for China. Prostitutes walked the streets looking worse for wear in the daylight. A woman approached the boys, smiled and offered them a special deal. They laughed at her and kept walking.

Two blocks west, Chinatown was burned to a crisp, with its wooden, close-quartered, tenement buildings. Loss of life was great here, but mostly undocumented by a city indifferent to the sufferings of this immigrant population. The smell of dim sum and roasted duck made Heath's mouth water. Asian men stir fried dishes and charged pennies for delicious meals. Heath ordered some pork fried rice while Joe got steamed pork buns, and they sat on a curb and shared.

They turned up California Street towards Nobb Hill, where the cable car tracks stood empty. Horse drawn wagons filled in as a poor substitute. The fire did not care that this part of town was rich. Redwood mansions burned as easily as slums. Yet, at the top of the hill, a single structure stood untouched. The fire had swallowed everything except this beautiful home with its Greek marble columns glistening in the sunlight; like a glutton who had eaten its fill and left only a choice piece of fillet on its plate.

Down the hill they marched on toward North Beach where Irish and Italian immigrants lived before the Earth's rupture. This area was also a wasteland with few buildings standing and heavy damage everywhere. In Washington Square Park, tents were pitched and laundry was hanging on lines to dry, fluttering in the breezy hazy daylight. Seagulls were diving at the garbage piled on the west side of the park. A priest was holding a funeral service on the north end of the park where the church used to stand. Nuns had gathered children into groups where they were teaching lessons as kids shared the few remaining primer books.

Finally, the boys found Mr. Angelo's warehouse near the bay waterfront. Inside the building was a beehive of activity. The father and the son briefly hugged.

"Have you eaten lunch?" The man asked.

Heath said, "We had a snack from a cart in Chinatown, but I'm still hungry."

"Come on," Alfred said.

They walked outside to the waterfront where an enterprising entrepreneur was selling sandwiches from a fishing boat. The meals had been made in Oakland and brought over to the hungry population on the western side of the bay.

"What do you want? I have salami, bologna, and ham," the man on the boat asked.

The sandwiches were already made and wrapped in newspaper. Each took one with a coke and settled down on the pier to eat. The bread was fresh Italian crusty sourdough and the meat was piled high.

"Dad, you wouldn't believe our house. There are people everywhere." The boy went on to describe his new living conditions.

"All things considered, I think you are one of the lucky ones." Mr. Angelo said and swung his arm pointing to the destruction of the smoldering city.

"I know I'm one of the lucky ones. It's just that...oh, never mind."

"I think you might have a crush on that seventeen-year-old Nobb Hill princess. What's her name?" Alfred said teasing his son.

"Lisa, ech, no way! It's just that she is using my bathroom and takes forever. Dad, she thinks she owns the place."

"Bet you two bits that you can't get her to kiss you before the summer is over."

Heath looked shyly at his friend Joe. One could almost see him thinking about the challenge. "Okay Dad, I'll take that bet." He smiled as he shook hands with his father.

It would be over two years before all the boarders were out of the Angelo house. By then San Francisco was well on its way towards reconstruction. Heath would win the bet, but could never prove it to his father, something they could rehash and laugh about years later.

SEPTEMBER 10, 1909

It was a warm sunny day in the East Bay, but Heath wore a blue blazer over his starched white shirt. Blue slacks led down to black socks and spit shined shoes. A blue bowtie completed the look of the freshman college student taking the commuter train up Shaddock Avenue to the University of California. Most of the students getting off the train were men dressed like young Mr. Angelo, but coeds were sprinkled in with their blue blazers, white blouses, and the ankle-length skirts.

The letter Heath held told him to report to North Hall for a nine a.m. geology class. The young man decided that earth science was his ticket to the future. He could look for the minerals and petroleum that he felt would lead to the modern inventions of the twentieth century. Of course, the earthquake also fed his curiosity and choice of major. If scientists could learn about its causation, maybe during this modern century, they could prevent the next catastrophe.

The rest of the schedule was filled with English, political science, and art history, all worthwhile endeavors he thought. Surprisingly the history of art class would become Heath's favorite, filling in a gap of his knowledge of a subject he knew just from his few visits to the now destroyed museum in San Francisco.

While the arts of the ancient Egyptians, Greeks, and Romans were interesting, as were the beautiful colors of the modern impressionists, what allured him the most were the Italian artists of the Renaissance? He wondered if he would ever get to Europe to see the works of art in person.

NOVEMBER 15, 1909

Heath was greatly disappointed. Professor Patrick Grey was droning on about his experience working with the hydro mining of gold in the Trinity Alps of northern California. While never having been there, Heath saw pictures of the unnatural disaster that the mining companies caused when using hoses to move massive quantities of earth to their enormous sloose boxes. The high pressured water would cause the erosion of beautiful mountainsides. Tons of earth and habitat would be displaced to get to the gold encased in the landscape. Dr. Grey seemed to be genuinely proud of his part in the destruction of the Trinity's natural beauty. He was a man stuck in the past. Like a Napoleonic general, he was encased in the nineteenth century. Nature was his enemy to be conquered and pillaged for its bounty.

The student met the professor after class hoping to learn more of the causes of the events of April 1906.

"Dr. Grey, I haven't found anything in your textbook. Do you know what causes earthquakes?"

The man looked at the boy making a face that appeared to have sucked a lemon. "That's not on your next test. You should be studying metamorphic rocks."

"I know sir. I'm ready for the exam, I'm just curious."

"No one knows what causes earthquakes. Only charlatans and gypsies claim to know about those things."

"Are you familiar with William Pikerings and William Taylor's hypothesis about moving continents and volcanoes?"

The look of distain by the professor told the student that he did not care about the writings of these men. "Mr. Angelo, I would suggest you spend more time studying rocks and fossils than reading these ridiculous theories about moving continents. If you want to know about volcanoes get yourself up to Mount Lassen and study igneous rock. My professor's assistant, Mr. Collins, will lead an expedition this summer."

Heath thought there was no way that he would want to spend time with that annoying Mr. Collins, that summer, but he politely thanked Dr. Grey for his time and left the classroom disheartened.

Only two years later, Alfred Wegner's continental drift theory was published, but was met with distain by most of the scientific circles. Yet, this theory was proven correct in the 1960's with the understanding of plate tectonics and its relationship to earthquakes and volcanoes. Later, Heath would read about these new scientific understandings and remember that old fool Professor Grey. The teacher had turned off the passion of his young student.

APRIL 15, 1910

Rachael Newberry held young Mr. Angelo's hand in the dark movie theatre. They played with each other's fingers as Heath's heart danced in his chest. Ms. Newberry had curls in her hair like her heroine, Mary Pickford, up on the silver screen. Rachael was in his art history class and they had spent time studying with each other holding up pictures of paintings to identify in their textbook. Heath thought she was the prettiest coed in the school. In class, the girl sat a row in front of him. He tried not to stare at her well-turned ankle below her long pleated skirt.

After the movie they went for espresso in the new shopping area on Telegraph Avenue. Berkeley had grown from a small town of a few hundred to a city of over forty thousand people after the earthquake in the early part of the twentieth century.

"I wouldn't be with you if I didn't care about you", the young woman said to Heath.

"But you would never leave him, would you?"

"I don't know what I want to do."

She was engaged to Arthur Felton, the oldest son of a rich Oakland banker. The gold ring on the brunette's finger belied her indifference.

"So let's change the subject. Will you go to the play with me Friday night? 'Romeo and Juliet' is playing at the Greek theatre on campus."

"Really, Heath, 'Romeo and Juliet'? Do you really want to see a play with me about star-crossed lovers?"

"Well, I didn't choose the fact that the drama department is doing that play. Besides, a rose by any other name would not look more beautiful or smell as sweet as you."

"God, you and Shakespeare are such silver-tongued devils."

"So will you go Friday night?"

His face scrunched up, then relaxed. "Okay, just this once."

He bent across the table and kissed her quickly.

Rachael waved a finger at him and said, "Don't you dare do that again." Rachael protested too much, but he knew she didn't mean it.

MAY 10, 1910

Class emptied out into the courtyard and Heath went to grab Rachael's hand. She retreated from him and sat on a concrete planter box facing her fellow art student. She looked pale in the bright sunlight, a frown fixed on her face. "We have set a date."

"What…? When….? No you can't! You love me."

"I never said that."

"But I can tell."

"I love Arthur and I will marry him."

"So the time you spent with me meant nothing?"

"No, I care deeply about you."

"It's because he is rich, right?"

"Heath, don't do that. I was engaged to him before I ever met you. I love him."

He didn't believe her.

"I can't study with you anymore." She said. "It would be too hard."

The woman wiped tears from her eyes with the left sleeve of her blouse.

Heath could feel mist coming to his eyes but he swallowed hard. He would be damned if he would let her see him cry.

"This would be goodbye then." He said.

"I'll see you at exams next week."

Heath turned his back on the girl. His heart ached. He felt dizzy like he did during the earthquake aftershocks, but he kept walking away from his first love.

Young Mr. Angelo would never return to classes at the University of California, Berkeley. He was disillusioned as a student and disheartened at love. Today, the University of California has been deeded the preserve that bears his name. I think he would be happy that the science department he once attended uses his land to do the type of scientific study that Professor Grey could never understand.

FEBRUARY 20, 1915

He was bigger than life, the most famous man in the world, Theodore "Teddy" Roosevelt. The former president of the United States was in San Francisco for the World Fair. Teddy was making good on a promise he had made during his administration. After surveying the damage from the earthquake and fire, he agreed to attend these festivities.

The city was ready for him and the world. A modern twentieth century metropolis arose from the ashes. The fairgrounds along the bay stretched from the Embarcadero to Fort Mason with exhibits from thirty-one nations. Just one of the exhibits, the palace of machinery, was the biggest building ever created and had one of those new aeroplanes fly through it. Electric Lights, another new invention, beamed into the sky with every color from the rainbow. Henry Ford even built a real Model-T assembly line for his exhibit.

Thrust upon this spectacular circus atmosphere was a young woman of the twentieth century, Betina Angelo, a reporter for the San Francisco Examiner. It was this new bride's job to interview the former president.

Heath accompanied his wife to the grand opening ball that evening. She was wearing a black silk dress in the new style of a modern suffragette, only coming halfway down her lower leg. One could see the seams of her black silk stockings above her ankles. The shortness of her hemline would have been a scandal only a few years earlier. White pearls were strung around her lovely twenty year old neck and her new gold ring was lovingly placed on her left hand. Her husband wore a tuxedo with long tails and white tie, more formal attire than his wedding day.

The paper arranged a ten-minute interview with the elder statesman, thinking he would be more amicable with a beautiful young woman than an older, more seasoned male reporter.

"Are you nervous?" Heath asked his wife.

"Hell yeah! But I'm ready. I've got my list of questions."

"This is quite a shindig. I've never seen anything like it."

"I know. I just saw the mayor with the senior senator from California."

"By the way, Mrs. Angelo, did I say that you are the most beautiful woman in the room?"

"You really know how to flatter a girl. You clean up pretty well yourself." She laughingly said. "But you look a little uncomfortable in that tux."

He laughed with her. "Oh, this monkey suit? I used to wear it all the time in the factory." He pulled at his shirt collar. "Wasn't it wonderful walking along the bay and looking at all the pavilions?"

"Yes, this fair is incredible!"

Betina took his hand and steered him to the dance floor. She held him close; her head on his shoulder, acting like a newlywed.

They met when she went to Angelo and Son Box and Basket Company offices at the North Beach warehouse to interview his father. It was part of a series that the paper was doing on successful businessmen in the city. That was one of Betina's first assignments. The young woman had been assigned to the city social desk, one level below the society page. The female reporter was interviewing Alfred when she noticed Heath. He smiled at the young woman and tipped his cap, then walked back outside the office to continue his project.

"Is that the son from Angelo and Son?" She asked.

"Yeah. You want to meet him?" Alfred asked, noticing her interest.

"Sure, why don't we make him part of the interview."

Heath came in and sat down. She thought he was cute with his open collar blue cotton work shirt and red striped suspenders that contrasted with his father's button-down white shirt and bowtie. The two flirted through the rest of the interview, which amused Alfred. Being a modern woman, she asked Heath out to lunch.

Heath smiled, "No, I don't think so. I'll only go out with you if you let me buy you dinner."

Betina's blue eyes danced. "Okay, dinner it is. When?"

"Are you free tonight?"

"I have no plans after I file my story."

"Give me your address and I'll pick you up at seven. Okay?"

"Dress?"

"I'll wear a white shirt, tie and jacket. I'll let you take it from there."

Heath thought she looked beautiful, wearing a red blouse and matching black skirt and jacket. He took her to a steakhouse just south of Market Street. He had a t-bone. She had a small fillet. They both had too much red wine. He kissed her goodnight at the door. "Will I see you again?" He asked.

"How about tomorrow?"

The two quickly fell in love and the wedding took place before Christmas.

"The President will see you now," the aid said to Betina, bringing her back to the present. Mr. and

Mrs. Angelo walked over to the main table and saw the familiar figure of the elder Teddy Roosevelt. The former president stood and shook the hand of the reporter. He smiled at Betina, putting her a little bit at ease.

"So you have some questions for me. I'm glad to speak to my friends at the Examiner. They couldn't have picked a lovelier representative. The woman's cheeks turned scarlet under the gaze of the older man.

"Thank you, Mr. President. Let's start with your impression of the fair and the progress of San Francisco since the last time you were here in 1909."

"It's bully! The fair is incredible. San Francisco should be proud of this exhibition but even more proud of the rebuilding of this metropolis."

"You were very critical of your successor Mr. Taft. What do you think of the Wilson Administration's progress on what you used to call a fair deal for the American people?"

"Well, in spite of being a Democrat, I think he has been a good Progressive. The amendments on the direct election of senators and women's suffrage are very welcome."

"So you are looking forward to women voting in national elections?"

The old man chuckled. "When someone as lovely and as intelligent as you votes…well, that would be a good thing. I'm sure that I would have been elected in a landslide if women could have voted for me in 1912."

"Mr. President, you're a famous hunter and yet you have fought to create national parks and conservation. Do you see a contradiction there?"

"Please call me Teddy. I feel incredibly alive when I'm outdoors hunting. Yet, I love nature and all the wildlife. I've written books on native birds. If city people go hunting they will want to preserve the outdoors for the future. I'm as proud at creating the park lands as anything I've accomplished as President. My friend John Muir showed me the beauty of Yosemite here in California; those granite peaks and green valley will be there for the millennia. Have you been there?"

"No, Mr. Prez...I mean Teddy."

"Well, in two days my entourage will make a pilgrimage to those majestic mountains. I invite you and your husband to come with us."

Betina looked at Heath. Without almost a second's delay he said, "Mr. President, how can we say no? We would be honored."

"One last question Mr. President...er...Teddy. I need to ask you for my story. What about the war in Europe?"

He stood up and raised his voice, the hall becoming quiet as everyone turned their attention to the great man's impromptu speech. "I'm glad you asked. We were unprepared and that delayed our response when I marched up San Juan Hill against Spain in Cuba. I believe we should get our boys ready. We will fight and we should fight against the Kaiser after he invaded poor Belgium. I will campaign to get us off our duffs. Mr. Wilson is wrong. He is acting like a coward. We need a national draft now."

People in the ballroom, even if they were not sure if they agreed with him, stood and cheered the "Old Bull Moose". His charisma was overwhelming.

"Thank you Mr. President." Betina said and shook Teddy's hand. She turned to her husband and said, "I need to go file my story. I'll meet you back at the apartment. Okay?"

"I'll get you a cab." Many of the cabs were still horse drawn coaches, mixed with more modern automobiles. Heath flagged down a carriage for his wife, and then boarded a streetcar to their south of Market Street apartment. He was still awake when Betina came home. He had changed out of his rented tuxedo and into his pajamas.

"Page one!" Betina screamed at him as she saw him sitting drinking a glass of bourbon."

"How wonderful! You were amazing, alive and alluring. Mrs. Angelo, come to bed."

Betina took off the necklace and carefully laid it on the dresser. She let him unbutton her dress and it fell to the floor. He replaced the pearls with kisses on her neck and they fell into bed laughing like little kids on the playground.

FEBRUARY 25, 1915

Snow shrouded the trees turning the whole valley into a big Christmas card. Sunlight exploded in the colors of the rainbow as light refracted off the wind-blown dustings of powdered snow from the ponderosa pine tree needles. Yosemite Falls was frozen stiff, not flowing but big icicles hung down replacing the water. El Capitan's granite cliff shimmered below a layer of white.

Heath had been here once before, camping with his parents and had been awed by the beauty of the valley, but he had never seen anything like this. Betina walked along the valley trail next to the Merced River, awed by the beauty, not feeling the cold as the sun lowered its golden light through the mountain passes. Tears came to her eyes, the wind and sunlight reflecting the snow almost blinded her from the amazing views. The presidential party walked ahead of the newlyweds leaving them alone, as they walked gloved hand in hand.

"Heath, it's magic. I would not be surprised if angels appeared flying down from the tops of the peaks."

"Magnificent." Was all he could say.

"I can see why Mr. Roosevelt is so proud to have preserved this place."

"Betina, it's beautiful in summer but this is special. We're so lucky to be here right after a winter storm. Wow!"

The paper had agreed to pay for the trip; happy to have an exclusive with Betina keeping a journal to report back to the Examiner about Teddy Roosevelt's trip back to the park he created.

The journey to Yosemite took two days, leaving Oakland by train, taking them to the lumber camps at Mariposa, where they stayed overnight. The entourage boarded a small gage steam train following the Merced River all the way to the park. Horse drawn wagons brought the group and their equipment to the valley floor where workers went ahead to set up tents and camping equipment. The wagon stopped halfway to camp to let those who wanted to walk the last five miles. Of course, the President was the leader of the group that walked.

Five large campfire rings were already ablaze, greeting them as they approached the tented grounds. A man with a clipboard assigned them to their tents. They would be separated. The eight women on the trip were segregated from the men, in spite of their married status. Seven were wives of the dignitaries and much older than Betina but a senator's daughter was nineteen and gravitated to Heath's young wife.

Heath was assigned to tent fifteen and he ducked under the flap to see sixteen cots set up military style with eight on each side. Large goose down sleeping rolls were spread neatly on top of each cot with their luggage neatly placed by their beds.

The sunset quickly in the mountains and cold enveloped the valley. Betina and Heath huddled under a wool blanket close to the outer west side campfire. Stewards served the guests a gourmet meal of grilled stuffed fresh trout, roasted game hens, pan grilled, and corn cooked in their husks. The couple could not remember ever having a tastier meal. From his camping days of childhood with his parents, Heath could remember how good simple hamburgers and hot dogs tasted outdoors. As dessert of apple pie was delivered, the former president made his way to their campfire.

"Hello Mr. and Mrs. Angelo. I hope you're enjoying my park. Isn't it just bully?"

"Magnificent, Mr. President, I mean Teddy." Betina replied as the couple stood to meet the great man.

"I'm afraid I don't handle the cold as well in my advancing years as I did when I was a young cow hand in Montana." He leaned in and said softly with a laugh. "I've got two pairs of long underwear." Then he stood upright and continued, "Are you two going to join us for the hike tomorrow? Unfortunately the fresh snow will not allow us to go to the higher peaks."

"We are looking forward to it Mr. President." Heath said.

"Well goodnight you two." And Teddy disappeared into the darkness.

"Can you believe he remembered our names?" Betina asked her husband.

"I bet he remembers the beautiful women."

"You just know how to say the right things, don't you?" She leaned over and kissed him.

Heath put up his hands, soaking in the heat from the campfire. "I bet people remember Teddy more for all of this than they will for his Nobel Peace Prize and the Great White Fleet."

MAY 7, 1915

The naked woman sat in her hotel room drinking tea as strong and dark as her usual coffee. Heath smiled blissfully at her across the table. Their feet were up as they looked out a picture window, curtains open, to look down at a view of London's Thames River. The docks were full of ships loading military supplies to be sent to the troops facing the Germans in the Great War's trenches in France. The Examiner's owner, William Randolph Hearst, had read Betina's exclusive journal articles about Teddy Roosevelt in Yosemite. He was impressed, so he sent her to England to interview Britain's Prime Minister Herbert Henry Asquith. Mr. Hearst was not a neutral party. His relentless editorials encouraged the United States to declare war on Germany and enter the effort to make the world safe for democracy. Betina's husband accompanied the reporter, making the trip a late honeymoon.

He could also do some business trying to secure contracts with English companies for boxes and baskets. Business for Angelo and Son was booming. Boxes were needed to send the tons of American munitions to England, France, and even Germany. The United States had pledged neutrality and championed freedom of the seas; but Germany's submarine fleet made shipping to the allies dangerous.

Their journey took two weeks leaving on an American cruise ship from San Francisco through Teddy Roosevelt's new Panama Canal, then across the extensive expanse of the North Atlantic. They felt safe; the U-boats had never attacked a civilian ocean liner. Even when they attacked cargo ships, the submarines almost always surfaced and allowed unarmed ships to send its crew to lifeboats. Indeed, the Angelo's ship had a safe voyage to London, arriving on the fourth of May.

The prime minister's interview was scheduled for the evening of the seventh; giving the couple a few days to sight see. The first day, they took a horse drawn coach across the famous London Bridge to the Tower of London, where poor Anne Bolen lost her head. Next, they passed Big Ben and Parliament. They finished their day at the National Museum where Heath found some of the paintings he had learned about in his Berkeley art history class. The couple's romantic dinner was disappointing. The English cooking was horribly bland compared to the fine restaurants of San Francisco.

On day two of their working vacation, the two took the train to Stratford on Avon. Being a writer, Betina had to make a pilgrimage to the quaint village of William Shakespeare's home. The couple walked hand in hand on the quiet street where the Great War seemed very distant.

On the morning of May seventh, the honeymooners awoke to a gray London sky of rain out their window. Betina thought about her luck. She was married to a man she loved, and had a successful career as a reporter; everything she wanted. She awoke her husband that morning by reaching over with her polished fingernails and scratched his back, sending chills cascading down his spine. He giggled awake and kissed Betina all over her body. They made love. Unbeknownst to the happy couple, Heath planted a seed of discontent for their future. Finally, about two in the afternoon, they showered and dressed to go for a late lunch. They left the hotel and walked south to a small tearoom recommended by the concierge.

"EXTRA EXTRA READ ALL ABOUT IT. GERMAN SUBS SINK THE LUSITANIA!" A newspaper boy yelled to the crowd walking in the wet, yet sunsplashed streets.

"Holy hell!" Heath yelled, sucking in a breath. He looked at his reporter wife as her mind went over the consequences of the boy's exclamation.

"We'll take two papers." Betina said, taking one and giving the other to her husband.

They entered the tea room, barely looking up from the London Times articles.

"Table for two." Heath said to the waitress and she showed them where to sit in the cute quaint tea room they barely noticed. White bread sandwiches arrived cut neatly in quarters, lying on their sides with toothpicks in each section holding the bread and ham together. They ate unconsciously in silence, eyes glued to the papers. Finally Betina looked up and said, "This changes everything. I have to go to 10 Downing Street or Parliament to find the prime minister, anywhere I can find his aid."

"I'll go to check on our ship's accommodations back home. I wonder if they will even sail." Heath said blankly.

"Okay, we'll meet back at the hotel later. Bye honey." The woman quickly departed, a quick kiss preceding her footsteps.

Western Union Telegram:
7 May 1915. 1820 hours. London Time.
0920 Pacific Daylight Time.
From: Betina Angelo
To: San Francisco Examiner
Exclusive Report from London

Lusitania torpedoed by U-boat that never surfaced.
Went down in minutes off coast of Ireland. Stop.

Great loss of life on civilian ocean liner including women and children. Many missing. Stop.
Thousands march in the streets. Hang Kaiser in effigy. Stop.
Exclusive from prime minister to the Examiner:
Civilian shipping will continue. Stop.
Ships to be escorted by military convoys. Stop.
Ships to be delayed and rescheduled without public disclosure. Stop.
Attack on Gallipoli against the Ottomans will continue. Stop.
British army will be resupplied reinforced and reorganized in France. Stop.
P.M.'s cabinet to be reorganized after artillery shell scandal. Stop.
He claims Britannia still rules the seas and U-boats will be hunted with new weapons. Stop.
He asked San Francisco to encourage American government to help the British war effort. Stop.
He asked Germany to respect civilian ships. Stop.

Western Union Reply
From: Editor, San Francisco Examiner
To: Betina Angelo
0925 Pacific Daylight Time
You have front page in all Hearst papers. Stop.
Keep up the good work. Stop.

JULY 14, 1915

It took Heath and Betina six weeks to get back from London. Their return trip home was canceled. The two booked passage on an American steamer to New York. The S.S. Patterson carried cargo and passengers simply, no frills, but meals were included with the crew. The ship had to wait ten days for a convoy to form, forty civilian ships of all varieties with a military escort. A convoy can only move as fast as the slowest ship and the old Polish cargo ship, Gadankze, steamed at only eight knots. The group zigzagged across the Atlantic in heavy seas.

Betina was happy that the food was terrible because most of it found its way over the rail, half from the pitching of the sea and the rest from morning sickness. Heath could eat anything and felt comfortable in the rolling and dipping of the steam ship, maybe because of his experience with the unstable earth. The long, miserable trip seemed almost worthwhile when the convoy pulled into New York Harbor and the Statue of Liberty came into view. Betina, overwhelmed by emotion, hugged Heath and cried on his strong shoulder.

The sea wary couple checked into the Waldorf-Astoria Hotel with Hearst's New York Morning Journal picking up the tab. Showers, clean clothing, and a good meal on firm dry land did wonders for their dispositions.

Betina sat across from her husband at a fine Italian restaurant across from Central Park. She looked at him tentatively. "Honey, I think I'm pregnant."

"Really? That's wonderful! How do you know?"

"I'm late, and I'm never late."

He took her hand and kissed it. She smiled at the man who would be her baby's father.

"Are you ready to be a Papa?"

"Absolutely. Are you ready to be a mother?"

"I think so, but I'm so glad we've had a chance to take this trip first."

"I know, I have so much work to catch up with. My dad left a telegraph for me at the hotel saying hurry back, business is booming, and there is lots of work for me to do."

"Heath, can I ask you something?"

"Yes, of course."

"Are you happy?"

The man smiled at his wife. "Very. How 'bout you?"

"Yes, I'm happy. I have a great career, I love you, and I'm about to be a mom…but I have this feeling like things are going too perfect."

"You call that trip across the ocean perfect?" He said with a laugh.

She smiled, but still felt a little concerned about something. What? She did not know.

The next morning, the Californians boarded a train across the continent. They were overawed by the pine and hardwood covered Appalachians, the long expanse of the Great Plains, and of course, the purple mountain's majesty of the Rockies.

Betina was greeted warmly when she walked into the newspaper room.

John Wilson, the editor, said to his best female reporter, "Great job. Welcome home."

"Thanks. I have some great news for you." She said excitedly. "I'm pregnant."

She saw the color go out of his face. The man frowned and said, "Are you sure?"

"Yes." She said apprehensively. "I saw the doctor yesterday."

"Betina, I'm going to have to let you go."

"What?" She said incredulously. "I thought you said I did a great job."

"I did and you have a big bonus coming, but we need our reporters to be ready to drop everything for a story; to go out to the war or out into the middle of the night. It was one thing when you were single, but now you are married to a husband with a successful business and you're going to have a baby. Go home; get out of the rat race. It's your turn to be a momma."

"But I'm a great reporter. I know it. You said so yourself."

"Baby, I hate to loose you, but you can't stay here. Mr. Hearst is quite clear about that."

Anger, red-hot rage hit her like a slap in the face. The early twentieth century was no place for a married career mother.

"Take that bonus and shove it up Mr. Hearst's ass." She hissed, and walked out of the building, tears streaming down her face. The woman knew that the conflict in Europe was not her war. Getting the vote for women was not enough; this young suffragette was just starting her lifelong fight for women's rights.

JANUARY 1, 1924

Heath Jr., age nine, shared a room with his little brother Ulysses. They lived on the second floor of a walk-up apartment on Fremont Street just south of Market, close to San Francisco Bay. Being the oldest, Junior had the top bunk and from his room he could hear his parents fight, which they did often for as long as he could remember.

The morning light filtered through the fog and into the window of the boys' room. Ulysses had been up for awhile, playing with his toy fire engine. The younger boy tried to stay quiet but he knocked over the house made of wood blocks with the truck's extension ladder.

"Shush!" Junior said in a loud whisper, not wanting to wake his parents and restart the yelling from last night. "Come on Ulysses." He said to his five year old brother who was clad in red one-piece pajamas, complete with a button butt-flap in the back. Heath Jr. was wearing more mature night clothing, pajamas including separate pants and a shirt with a collar and breast pocket.

"Sit there." The older boy whispered pointing to a chair at the kitchen table and he grabbed corn flakes from the pantry and milk from the icebox to make breakfast for the two of them. Heath Sr. appeared holding two packed suitcases.

"Going somewhere, Dad?" Junior asked.

The father looked surprised to see his sons awake, chomping on the cereal. He had been hoping to avoid this scene.

"Boys, I'm going to spend some time with grandpa. I'll be back to see you in a few days."

The elder boy knew this was coming. The New Year's Eve argument became more intense between his parents as more alcohol was added to the combustible mix of their relationship. The subject of the fight neither participant could remember, but the oldest son could overhear how it ended.

Heath Jr. had overheard his mom yell, "You son of a bitch, I can't stand this anymore! I want you out of here."

Heath looked at his wife through bloodshot eyes. He almost felt relieved that she wanted him gone from the apartment. He took a blanket and went to grab a few hours sleep on the couch.

Betina never got over losing her career. She grew frustrated being a housewife while her husband went off the work at his successful business. While the woman did not blame him, he became a target of her wrath. Heath had supported Betina in her campaign for women's equal rights in the workplace. He even hired an attorney to see if a lawsuit was actionable about her unfair dismissal. The young wife wrote letters to congressmen, senators, and state officials, but William

Randolph Hearst was not the man you wanted to pick as an enemy. He had unlimited funds, a newspaper empire and a team of attorneys defending any chance of Mrs. Angelo being successful politically or judiciously. When Heath gave up the campaign, Betina started to see her partner as part of the problem.

The young father took a cab to Albert's apartment near the warehouse where his dad had made up a rollaway bed. After the son was settled in, the two went out to a neighborhood diner for breakfast. They sat devouring eggs, ham, and fresh French sourdough bread with lots of butter.

"Dad, why did you leave mother?"

"It wasn't just one thing. We fought over every little thing. I guess we just fell out of love."

"I always thought that maybe I did something to drive you away. If I could do my chores better or something...you would quit fighting."

The elder Mr. Angelo was quiet for a moment, looking out on the bay and back in time. "You don't still think that it was your fault, do you?"

"No, of course not, but I want to make sure the boys don't think that our fighting is their fault."

"What do you and Betina fight about? I always thought that you were a great couple."

Heath gave an ironic laugh. "What don't we fight about? I think she has become a very unhappy woman...especially unhappy with me."

Albert smiled knowingly. He said with a laugh, "Have you tried flowers?"

"There are not enough roses in the world to cure her blues. I don't think she ever got over being fired. Somewhere in the back of her mind she blames me for getting her pregnant and having to give up her career; not consciously, but deep inside resentment."

"Well Sigmund Freud, I think you've got that figured out."

"Except I wasn't a good enough shrink to cure us."

"You still hung-over from last night's New Years Eve's debacle?" The father asked.

The son instinctively rubbed his temples. "A little."

"Come on, let's get you some hair of the dog."

MAY 20, 1924

Kathryn Erickson walked into the Speak Easy and male heads turned. She wore a black silk fringed "flapper" dress that came down just below her knees. Her long legs were covered with sheer silk stockings, with red pumps completing her outfit. The woman was made more striking with her fashionably short, straight platinum blonde hair. Beads hung down below her cleavage, accentuating her ample breasts. It seemed like a spotlight shined on Miss Erickson, while her pretty brunette companion was lost in her shadow.

Heath was at a bar with his employee and friend, Timothy. The still young Mr. Angelo was drinking good Canadian whiskey. Part of his shipment he had delivered to the not so secret Falcon Nightclub on Columbus Street.

San Francisco during prohibition stayed very wet. A full eighty-three percent of the city had voted against the eighteenth amendment in 1914 and the people found plenty of illicit bars in which to satisfy their thirst.

Unlike New York and Chicago, gangs and bosses never dominated the import and manufacture of alcohol in the Northern California city. Underground supplies of wine came from vineyards in the Central Valley and the huge coastline was open to any free agent who could afford a boat. Heath had two lumber ships that allowed him to import the illicit elixir from Canada, hidden below the logs. The local police were happy to look the other way. Of course the Feds were always a danger, but they had bigger fish to fry.

After picking out her prey, Kathryn walked right up to Heath and said confidently, "If you buy me a drink, I'll dance with you."

The man smiled shyly at her, "Lady, I'm just sitting here enjoying this good whiskey and listening to the jazz band." The fact that he didn't just snap to attention intrigued her all the more.

"Oh no you don't, get off your butt and dance with me!" She grabbed his hand and almost dragged the new divorcee to the dance floor. The woman tried to lead him through the paces as the band played a swinging Charleston. He tried not to step on her high-heeled feet. When the song was finished and the buzz died down, the two young ladies came to sit with Heath and his friend.

"Now you owe me a drink." Kathryn said.

"I don't even remember agreeing to the dance." But Heath signaled over the waitress and the girls ordered gin fizzes. The mixed drink was a perfect way to hide the taste of bad bathtub gin.

Heath said, "I recognize a little accent. Is that Norwegian?"

"Actually, my parents are Swedish, but I'm from Minnesota and staying here in the city with my friend, Susie." She said, nodding to the woman in the other seat. "We grew up together and when she wrote me how much fun San Francisco was, I had to come join her. Of course my parents were furious. They are old-fashioned farmers."

Heath asked her "So what do you do here?"

"Well, Susie is a secretary and I'm looking for a job." She whisked back her bangs from her beautiful blue eyes and batted her false eyelashes, openly flirting with the man across from her. She was hard to ignore. "Sorry, I didn't get your name."

"Heath...Heath Angelo." He extended a hand to shake.

She took it lightly almost caressing it. "My name is Kathryn Erickson but please call me Kate. What do you do for work?"

"I have my own business." Heath left it at that. He was wearing black trousers and a white starch shirt but his top collar was unbuttoned and his black and red striped tie was loosened a little. His tweed jacket sat over the seat.

"I thought I was going to freeze coming here. The fog almost went right through me. Sometimes I think I was warmer in Minnesota...well, maybe not in mid-winter, but its cold here.

He smiled at her novice reaction to the cold, windy, summer nights of San Francisco. The young woman leaned forward showing him her cleavage.

"Come on, let's dance." In spite of his reluctance, he found himself being led back onto the dance floor as a snare drum laid down the beat and the saxophone sounded sexy. Heath walked the damsel home, his jacket over her bare shoulders, so he had to brave the wind.

"I see you're not wearing a ring, how come a good looking guy like you is single?" Kate asked, holding his left hand.

"Just divorced. I have two sons. What about you, no boyfriend back home?"

She laughed. "I had a childhood sweetheart and he asked me to marry him but it just didn't feel right. I wanted to get out of Brainerd.

She allowed him to kiss her goodnight. "May I call on you again?" He asked.

She said with a smile on her face "Yeah sure, you betcha," in her best Swedish-Minnesota accent.

Heath walked home unsettled. He did not want to get involved with a woman so quickly after his divorce, but her perfume lingered on his jacket and Miss Erickson was already lingering in his head.

JULY 4, 1924

It was a glorious day. Heath and Kate took a streetcar down Geary Street to the beautiful Victorian Cliff House for lunch. Huge picture windows looked out on a view of the crashing ocean waves exploding against the rocky coast. Men were dressed in ties and jackets while women wore fancy dresses and fine jewelry. Kathryn looked like a Hollywood starlet with her white, short flapper dress against her pale skin. Mr. Angelo ordered roast beef and his lady had turkey, both fresh-carved at the table by a tuxedoed waiter. The early afternoon sun made the fog retreat west allowing the couple to watch the seals frolic in the waves below the coastal rocks. After eating quietly, Kate demurely wiped her mouth and said, "This place is breathtaking. I don't think I've been anywhere so beautiful. Thanks for taking me." She leaned over and kissed his cheek.

"I would watch the view but I don't want to take my eyes off of you. You look amazing." He kissed her hand. "Ready for a walk?"

"Lead on, handsome."

They went down the steep hill to the beach. Wind whipped off the water, and Kathryn was glad Heath warned her to bring a sweater, but they couldn't resist taking off their shoes to walk barefoot in the sand. They turned after a half hour and made their way back up the hill, past the Cliff House to the Sutro indoor bathhouse. They parted to go change to their swimsuits and when they reunited the two held hands, jumping into the heated salt water. An elaborate system pumped the water in from the ocean below.

Kate splashed at him playfully and he grabbed her, pushing her head down below the water for a second. She came up spitting salt water in his face, and they both laughed.

He yelled over the din, "I'll get you!"

She screamed, sprinting away with the powerful strokes she learned growing up swimming in the summers in the land of ten thousand lakes. She purposely slowed down so she could let him catch her and they could kiss passionately out of breath.

Back at the North Beach Pier that evening, Miss Erickson and Heath sat on one of the company's logging boats. Fireworks were exploding over the bay and the two were necking, their passion matching the explosions in the air.

"Slow down, Tiger." Kate said breathlessly, removing his hand from the top of her dress. Heath felt like he was caught up in a whirlwind, almost dizzily in love with this blonde temptress.

"I love you Kate. Marry me." He heard himself say.

"Oh yes, yeah, yes!" She said shocked by the suddenness of the invitation. She kissed him all over his face as the fireworks in the sky reached a crescendo. The two lovers went down below deck and fell into each other's arms.

AUGUST 15, 1924

The picadors were dressed in green jackets with stark white britches, looking like the colors of the Mexican flag. The wide-brimmed hats were big enough to block the bright sun from their eyes and they were tied tightly to their chin with leather straps. The beautiful horses were adorned with green blankets and ribbons under the saddles and they pranced, legs marching high like the toy soldiers in the Nutcracker ballet. The picador horse parade was choreographed with the blue coated toreadors marching not like marines, but with a graceful gait. The horsemen showed a combination of styles, hundreds of years of Spanish tradition, mixed with the riding precision of the Mexican vaquero. The beautiful pageantry was breathtaking.

Then, the bull entered the ring confused but proud, with a machismo to match the Mexican cowboys. Only then did Kate and Heath notice the spear that each picador held. The horsemen were trained brilliantly for their task. Their mounts were now not just dancing, but flowing with the bull as each picador slid his spear into the bovine's neck. The red blood added to the colorful spectacle as each vaquero took his turn stabbing the bull.

The picadors disappeared, leaving the bull dazed and angry. From a side gate, the matador magically appeared, strutting into the rink and prancing like a peacock. His pants were pulled so skintight that his codpiece bulged like it was competing with the huge testicles of the bull, machismo versus machismo.

The matador bowed to the crowd, seemingly ignoring the beast in the ring. The bull turned his gaze to the solitary man, angrily snorting and pawing at the dirt, sending a dust cloud into the air. His blood glowed in the bright Mexican sunlight. Finally, the matador waved his cape at the bull hiding his lethal sword.

"TORRO, TORRO!" The seemingly small figure yelled.

The animal charged, horns lowered, ready to find flesh, but the graceful matador danced at the last second and horns found only the red cape.

"OLE!" The crowd yelled with the blood lust of Mark Anthony's mob. The battle raged, horns against cape, man against beast.

It was never a fair fight. The wounded bull grew tired…head and horns getting steadily lower…moving slower…out of breath. With each pass the crowd yelled, "OLE!" bracing them for the inevitable. In the end, the skillful dancing matador let his blade stab into the shoulders finding the heart of the animal and the blood flowed like a slaughterhouse. The matador bowed and waved in triumph. He cut the ears off and presented them to a fair maiden in the first row of the ringside.

Heath wrestled with his thoughts. Was this spectacle beautiful or horrible? Kathryn seemed to have no doubt as she screamed and cheered the blood-splattered victor in the ring, her blue eyes as big as saucers. Her blood flowing in her veins mixed with adrenaline. She hugged her husband, kissed him on the cheek, and squeezed his hand hard. Breathlessly, she said, "I've never seen anything like that in my life. We're a long way from Minnesota."

They were also a long way from San Francisco. They had come down the coast by train for a quick weeklong honeymoon in Tijuana, Mexico. The border city brought out the best and the worst of the two countries in the 1920's. Before Vegas could make that claim, what happened in Tijuana stayed in Tijuana. Gambling, prostitution, and a flow of legal booze mixed the millionaire with the bourgeoisie middle class of the Roaring Twenties America. The newlywed Angelos were met at the train station in San Diego by Pablo Martinez, who spoke good enough English to win a job at the Vista Grande Hotel to be their personal driver and guide. George Washington, Andrew Jackson, and Abe Lincoln were former presidents of the United States but in Mexico having their pictures in your wallet could make you a king. The price of a personal driver and guide was less for a day than Heath paid one of his workers by the hour back home. The two were escorted to the honeymoon suite of a beautiful Spanish-style veranda overlooking a sand-swept Pacific Ocean beach, just miles from downtown Tijuana. They took in the bullfight on their first full day in town.

Joey Adcock was tall for a jockey. At six foot two, he was rail thin. The nineteen-year-old red head could eat all day but nothing stuck to his boney frame. He had come to Tijuana down on his luck. Growing up on a ranch in Montana, he left home at fifteen after another drunk beat-down by his abusive father. Hitchhiking down the west coast, he worked his way down to Los Angeles, arriving without a nickel in his pocket. The one thing the boy could do was ride. He was in the saddle before he could walk, a true cowboy.

He found the racetrack and worked as a practice rider for two years, unable to get a mount in a race because he had no experience as a jockey. At eighteen he broke his maiden, but rookies don't get good horses, and losers don't get any mounts. He crossed the border for the track in Tijuana where he joined the other dead-enders trying to change his luck.

Joe could ride and among losers, he becamc a winner. By mid-season, the educated gambler learned to put their pesos on the slim, redheadcd gringo.

Maria Rosa Alvarez sat across from the jockey at a table in Club St. Louis in downtown Tijuana. She was the third straight girl born to her dirt poor Mazatlan family. All three girls were named Maria, but each with a different middle name. Being the third girl, her family called her Tres. Two more girls were born after her, so she was stuck in the middle. Her father felt unlucky, not having sons. She shared a silent secret with Mr. Adcock, she had left home after her alcoholic father beat her for spilling a milk pitcher on her awkward adolescent fifteenth birthday. There would be no quiencinera for this young senorita. She slipped out of her hovel before daybreak, heading north, hoping to cross into Estados Undidos to find work. Unable to get across the border, the pretty young descendent of an Aztec princess was able to find a job as a bar girl at Club St. Louis. She would get half the money of each drink she could find a gringo to buy for her. Maria was the only bar girl in the club who was still a virgin so she was not yet selling her body with the drinks, which kept her in poverty, living in a cheap back alley apartment. She liked this young gringo and was tempted to negotiate to get some of his hard earned winnings for sex.

Pablo drove Heath and Kathryn to downtown. The sun had just set and twilight glowed in the dust kicked up from street traffic. Downtown Tijuana in the early twentieth century almost looked like a scene out of the old west; burrows with baskets outnumbered the occasional car on the dirt avenues. The mostly one or two story wood or adobe buildings sported hand painted signs in Spanish and English, sometimes misspelled in a Spanglish.

Heath told his guide that they wanted to go to a fun club with dancing. Club St. Louis was on the corner of a main street. Pablo opened the door of the Ford Model T and the couple slid out and made their way into the double doors of the club. The name implied American jazz and as the newcomers' eyes adjusted to the dim kerosene lighting, they saw a "negro" jazz band playing in the corner. The six black friends had left New Orleans and the restrictive Jim Crow laws of the South two years earlier, to find a relative freedom playing music in the Mexican border town. The band included three horns, a stand up bass, a drummer, and a piano player which belted out as sweet a ragtime number as any good jazz band Heath ever heard in San Francisco. As the couple walked into the bar, every man, Mexican or American, turned to look at Kathryn. She was adorned in a floral linen dress pulled down Mexican-style so her shoulders were naked. Her tall marble statuesque beauty and blonde hair in the land of shorter, darker women made her stand out like a basketball player among jockeys.

Joey Adcock looked at her and his breath slipped away. Maria immediately resented the gringa with her fine dress and black high heels that would take her months of pay to afford. Pablo pulled out the seats at the table next to the jockey and his lady friend. The Mexican guide talked to the headwaiter, then turned to his charges and said, "My friends, you will be well taken care of."

"Do you want to join us?" Heath asked.

"No, no that would not be alright. I have a table in the back. They know me. Just wave for me and I will be here."

Margaritas appeared, with fresh still warm chips with guacamole and spicy salsa. Kate bit into a chip with salsa, her first taste of Mexican food. Heath laughed when she stood up like her mouth was on fire. Her nose ran and tears came streaming down her face, ruining her carefully crafted makeup. She swallowed some icy margarita, which only spread the fire, but did not put it out. Slowly, her mouth cooled.

"You had better stick with the guacamole." Heath said with a laugh.

"What the hell was that?!"

"Just some salsa. I was going to warn you that Mexican food is spicy."

"That's not spicy. Spaghetti is spicy. That is fire!"

"You said you aren't in Minnesota anymore."

"I'll say!"

"Try the seafood, it's delicious." A platter of lobster and shrimp in a garlic butter sauce had been brought to them.

She looked at him crinkling her nose. "You sure?"

"It's mostly garlic, just a little spicy." She tried it, just a little piece of shrimp on a chip.

"Yum!"

After they finished eating, two more margaritas appeared. The waiter said, "It's from the gentleman next to you."

The redhead raised his glass and smiled. "You two want the company of a fellow countryman?" he asked.

"Want company?" Heath leaned in and asked his wife.

"Sure, you know me, life of the party."

"Join us." Heath said.

Introductions were made and inquiries of home cities were exchanged from Minneapolis to Matzatlan.

"How well do you speak English?" Heath asked Maria.

"Just a little." Maria said.

Joey said for the girl, "She understands more than she can speak. So you're on your honeymoon. How long?"

"Just a week." Heath answered, taking a long sip of his margarita.

"Watch that." Joey warned. "The tequila they put in their drinks is powerful medicine. I've seen Americans dancing on the table one minute and rolled in a back alley the next. I've learned my lesson; I just stick to the cervesa."

The warning came just in time. Heath felt himself get lightheaded but Kathryn took another sip. "You'll protect me, won't ya darling'?" and she put her hand on Heath's.

"Come to the races. I'm on good horses in the third and fifth. You might make some money." The jockey said.

"Oh babe, that would be fun." The bride said.

"Thanks for the invite. We will check it out."

"Great." The tall skinny redhead said. "I can even show you the horses and the stalls and if I hear of a good horse, I'll give you a good tip."

The four drank and danced into the night. Pablo helped Heath and Kate stumble into the waiting car. When they got back to the hotel the husband held back his wife's hair as she let loose, heaving her guts into the toilet, shrimp, lobster and tequila. When she was done, he poured her into the bed. Unbeknownst to them, her regurgitation probably saved her a worse fate. Unlike Joey and Maria, they passed out and would have no sex that night.

AUGUST 16, 1924

The ghost of the great Aztec king Montezuma grabbed Heath on the morning the couple was supposed to go to the racetrack, taking his revenge out on the gringo. The microscopic amoeba in the Mexican water supply invaded the digestive system of the Californian, cursing him with dysentery. The only reason he wanted to get out of bed was to run to the toilet. Because of her letting loose the night before, Kate was spared the bug and looked repulsively at her partner like he had leprosy. Nursing skill did not come naturally to the woman, who wanted to continue the vacation with or without him.

"Go." He said simply.

So she went, off to the races. He had no clue, no feeling that he would never see her again. In his dysentery delusion Heath heard her depart, high heels clicking on the Mexican tile floor. The reddish tint of the tiles clashed with her light blue skirt that blended together through his fog hazed blood shot eyes.

Kathryn had no plans of leaving Heath that August morning. She cared about the man she married and enjoyed his company. He was a kind and attentive man, and a good lover. So why did she feel so empty? She was not in love and while the honeymoon was fun, something was missing. The thought of settling down, becoming a housewife and having babies depressed the young woman who had become the star of the illicit nightclub scene of San Francisco.

As Kate was being driven to the racetrack she felt an amazing sense of freedom, like a kid who wakes up ready to go to school and realizes it's Saturday. Pablo took the young Mrs. Angelo to the Tijuana racetrack. "I'll be back for you at six o'clock," the guide said quietly to Mrs. Angelo.

"Thank you, Pablo." Kate said.

Joey walked up to Kathryn and asked. "Where is Heath?"

"Back at the hotel. He is sick with a bad stomach but wanted me to come and meet you and have a good time."

"Sorry he's sick, happens a lot here in Tijuana. So, are you ready for a day at the track? I'm riding in the third and fifth race, but can spend the rest of the day with you helping with your betting. It turns out this will be my last day here. I've been offered a place to ride at Santa Anita, just outside L.A."

Kate's eyes lit up. "Wow, Los Angeles, I've always wanted to go to Hollywood."

"Well, you're pretty enough to be a movie star."

"You really think so? That was always a dream of mine as a little girl growing up in Minnesota."

"Come on." Mr. Adcock said. "I've got a club seat reserved for you in the grandstands. I've heard the number two horse looks good in the first race. We should get a bet down."

As they moved to the seats she said, "This is so exciting!" and the lady planted a kiss on Joey's cheek, which he felt to his toes.

When Pablo came to pick up Mrs. Angelo at six, the woman was nowhere in sight. He waited an hour at the gate and when she did not show up, he was very worried. It was not unusual for an American woman to disappear in Tijuana, but it had never happened to him or anyone from the hotel. Her life and his livelihood were on the line. Yet he didn't want to get the police involved. He had his connections and he knew the downtown well. He would conduct a full search before going back to the hotel.

The seafood restaurant northwest of town by the Pacific was little more than a shack. Three adobe walls sat under a roof of corrugated steel and an ocean breeze blew through the opened end, cooling the interior of the modest abode. Straw thatched tables and chairs sat on the dirt floor. The sun still glowed hot as it lowered to the West over the water in the evening sky.

Kate was famished. She skipped breakfast and didn't trust the food from the vendors at the racetrack. The waiter was dressed in a white cotton shirt, linen slacks and sandals and he brought a tray filled with grilled shrimp, lobster, and vegetables. Joey showed the novice how to place all the fresh sizzling ingredients on a hot corn tortilla, then rolling it together. The Minnesota native bit into this heavenly combination of tastes and spices. Her taste buds exploded in an oral orgasm of flavor.

Joey was enraptured by his companion's beauty and charisma. He had no idea that she had purposely missed her ride back to the hotel. "You sure were my good luck charm today." The tall jockey won the third race and rode in the money placing, second in the fifth race.

"I was the lucky one." she said. "I took your tips and won almost three hundred dollars." She used her winnings to hatch her plan. Kathryn leaned forward knowing full well that the young man across from her could see down her blouse, teasing him with the sight of the top of her breasts. She smiled flirtatiously and touched his arm. "Take me to L.A. with you."

"What?!" He asked knowing that she was looking into his eyes, which were aimed down her neckline, in spite of himself. He quickly focused back to her blue eyes, now filling with tears, showing an acting ability she would later summit in her movie roles.

"He beats me. I need to get away…tonight."

"But you seemed like such a happy couple last night."

"He wanted you to think that."

"I wasn't planning on leaving till tomorrow…" He ran out of words.

"Oh please, you're my only hope. You have to get me out of here. If he found out we were having dinner together, he might kill me." Why was Kathryn making up these lies about Heath? She didn't even know. She just knew she wanted to go to Hollywood and this may be her only ticket. With her winnings she could get an apartment. She didn't want to be married, have children, be a wife. She just felt it, without thinking. It was so much easier to walk away than go back and talk to the man that cared about her.

"Okay" the jockey finally said. "I'll take you."

Heath woke up in a cold sweat. The fever finally broke. His stomach felt like it was tied in a huge knot. The man's immune system had battled millions of one-cell invaders. Leukocytes and the other body's natural defenses fought the attacking amoeba throughout the digestive system. Mobilized reserves were called in from the blood and by evening, Heath's defenses were winning, but his cell casualty count was in the millions. He felt weak; needing liquid to replenish his loses. The fresh orange juice left next to his bed tasted good, the first refreshment he had all day. The sunlight came through the west side window glaring directly into the man's face.

'Low in the sky, evening,' he thought. 'I've slept through the day. I wonder if there is any word from Kate.'

He picked up the black 1920's telephone, with the separate speaker and earpiece that sat quietly on the dresser beside the bed. He pulled down on the lever twice.

"Yes, sir." The man at the front desk answered in excellent English.

"This is Mr. Angelo in room 209. Is there any message for me from my wife?"

"No, sir. Pablo went out to meet her at five, but there is no word from him."

Heath looked at his pocket watch which lay next to the phone. The little hand pointed past six and the big one was on the eight. He wondered where she was but not greatly concerned. She probably went to get something to eat, which now sounded like a good idea. He felt empty and weak, fasting all day in his sickened state.

"Can you get room service to cook me up some eggs and toast?"

“Certainly, señor. The waiter will be up shortly.”

“Coffee too, okay?”

“Yes, sir.”

Heath staggered out of bed and pulled the curtains to dissipate the sunlight. After relieving his full bladder, he got into the shower. The water felt incredible, like it was bringing life to a fish washed up on shore.

Pablo was downtown. He and two friends had been making a systematic search looking for anyone who had seen the gringa. He thought the tall blonde would be easy to find, even in bustling Tijuana. As the sun went down, all his contacts reported that she had not been located anywhere in the city. He realized he must go back to the hotel and tell Senor Angelo that his wife was missing. She was last seen leaving the racetrack with Mr. Adcock. Before being the bearer of that bad news, he stopped at the police station, not to make an official missing person report, but to tell his friend on the force to make some inquiries.

Darkness engulfed the hotel. Only the light of the quarter moon sprinkled down, casting black shadows on three men as they sat on the back veranda.

Sea foam splashed as waves crashed against the rocks below. The beauty of the Baja scenery was lost on Heath as the waiter poured him another cup of the rich black coffee. The American was joined by the hotel manager and a captain from the Federales, Mexico's national police force. He looked at his pocket watch: half past eleven, the radium-painted arms glowed up at him. The men were eerily quiet, all the questions had already been asked, possibilities had been covered, and speculations discussed. Now they readied for a long night as agents explored the depths of Tijuana looking for the light-skinned woman. Pablo and his friend, the local policeman, walked across the patio approaching the trio. The men rose from the table.

Pablo spoke in English, "We have news, Mr. Angelo."

Heath nodded, waiting apprehensively.

The guide continued, "She was seen at the border with Mr. Adcock. They crossed into the United States."

The American fell back into his seat like he had been thrown down by the weight of gravity.

"Are you sure?"

The policeman spoke in English with a strong Spanish accent, "the border guard remembers a woman of her…what is the word?"

Pablo helped him, "Description."

"Yes." The man in the blue uniform continued. "Description. So our men checked with the border controls. The men, they say they remember her, checked her passport."

Heath sat in silence for a moment, looking out over the dark ocean, hearing the waves break against the shore, lost in thought. 'So she took her passport?'

He turned to the manager, "I'll check out tomorrow."

"Certainly, señor." Pablo can drive you to the train.

"Thanks for everything." The American offered each a tip of five American dollars, a lot of money in 1920's Mexico. They each took the money, although the two officers looked at each other and over their shoulders, a tip was not exactly kosher, yet under the table payments were common and even expected.

Back in his room the former honeymooner looked at his wife's clothing. What should he do with it? He started packing his own two suitcases, ignoring the dresses and undergarments belonging to Kathryn. It was well after midnight, but having slept all day and drinking many cups of coffee left him wide awake, staring up at the ceiling. 'Why did she leave? Why didn't she get her things? Why didn't she talk to me? What…?' He didn't even know the questions to ask himself. The affect of the dysentery abated, but his stomach still barked at him and his head throbbed. Finally, he drifted into a restless sleep.

In the morning Heath came down to the front desk and asked humbly if his wife had left any messages. There was no word. He then summoned Pablo to take him north to start his journey home. Kathryn's possessions stayed in the room, untouched, like she had never left. "Help yourself to her things." Heath told his guide, refusing to even speak the woman's name.

"Thank you, sir. They will be put to good use."

The Californian took one last look at the view, let out an audible sigh, and left Mexico behind, never to return.

OCTOBER 10, 1924

The boy pulled in the slack, his dad right behind him ready to take the rod, but instead giving encouraging instructions. Thc large white Albacore lurched away, almost pulling the fishing pole from the hands of Heath Jr.

"Give him some slack, let him run a bit."

The fish confused, frightened, swam until the line tugged and the hook bit through his gill. He turned and swam back towards the boat.

"Okay, now reel him in", the father instructed. "That's good. Hold on tight, he'll make another run."

The boy grimaced, ready for the jerk this time. The fish weighed more than the ten year old, but the boy was determined to bring him in.

It was a gorgeous California fall day, the sun glistening on the water. Without the fog and wind typical of summer, the seventy-degree day felt hot. Sweat gathered under the boy's San Francisco Seals baseball cap. They were beyond the Farallon Islands, with the Marin headlands in sight.

Heath Sr. felt good to be alive, to be out on the ocean with his sons. The sting of his failed romance was behind him like a truck he might pass at night on Highway 1. He could still see the taillights, but they were getting dimmer in his rearview mirror.

After he got home he received her letter:

Dear Heath,

I'm so sorry. I just could not face you. I was a coward and had to go. You know it wasn't you. I just couldn't see myself as a housewife with children running around and you already had two. I did not want to be a mother. Sorry. I thought I did. I think I loved you, but not enough. Mr. Adcock was going to Hollywood. I always wanted to be an actress. Now I have my chance.

Fondly, Kathryn

A quick annulment followed and the marriage was over. It seemed unreal, a weird dream, like he was a character in one of the motion pictures in which Kathryn would later star. The curtain came down and he walked out of the metaphysical theatre into the bright California sunshine. Now that it was over, he could look back at the romance with fondness and amusement.

"Get me the net, Ulysses!" the father said to the younger boy as Junior reeled the big fish closer to the same boat that he had watched the Independence Day fireworks with Kate just a few months earlier. 'Fireworks,' Heath would think. 'That's what Kate was like, exploding into his life, then gone from the daylight sky.'

"Wow, Junior, look at him, a beauty. We'll eat fresh tuna steaks tonight."

Heath turned the boat south and east, back through the open Golden Gate, before the bridge. A rebuilt San Francisco came into view, with Coit tower atop its hill, shaped like a fireplug to honor the men who fought the blaze after the earthquake. A smile worked its way to the father's face. He lived through an earthquake and two failed marriages. The man was happy to be alive, wondering what would come next.

NOVEMBER 12, 1924

Fate works in wondrous ways. If not for the wanderlust of Kathryn Erikson, a great love story would not have come to pass. California and the world would be missing the grandeur of a saved nature's bounty. Clear streams would not feed into the rushing waters of the Eel River. Majestic conifers would not reach up to the heavens, providing sanctuary for tiny birds and great brown bears. The mountain lions would have one less place to roam free and hunt the whitetail deer of Northern California.

Now that they were no longer married, Betina and Heath became good friends, forming a parental alliance for their two sons. When his former wife invited Heath to a Sierra Club meeting, he was happy to accompany her.

A battle was being fought. People were "being cool" with President Calvin Coolidge, but not the conservationists of California. Yosemite Valley was in danger of becoming another Hetch Hetchy, damned and providing water for agriculture, hydro-electricity and a growing thirsty population. Opposing the administration was the legacy of John Muir, the Sierra Club, fighting to keep the home of Half Dome from becoming an unnatural lake. The organization was on a campaign to convince the newly elected President to conserve the valley.

Betina and Heath met near Broadway and took the cable car through Chinatown to the top of Knob Hill, disembarking in front of the newly completed and elegant Fairmont Hotel. The two walked into the magnificent high-ceiling lobby, and then took an elevator to the restaurant at the top floor, where the conservation organization was meeting. From the elegant dining room, the picture windows showed an incredible view of the rebuilt city. It was a clear evening and looking east, Heath could see past his childhood home of Alameda Island to the top of the Oakland hills, covered in second-growth Redwood trees. Members of the Sierra Club helped maintain trails in those hills where he spent many hours hiking.

A buffet of roast beef, baked potatoes, and green beans was on the menu, with most of the dinner's profits going to the political action committee. The formerly married couple was at a table of eight. Everybody introduced themselves. Jack Crain was an officer in the local club chapter, and a branch manager for Bank of America. Larry Murry worked at the shipyards. Cynthia Segal was a third grade teacher. Linda and Steve Cryer were married for twenty-three years. He drove a bus and she was a housewife with three boys.

“We have two boys together.” Betina said, and laughed explaining. “We were married and now we are just friends and co-parents.”

“How does that work?” the pretty woman who just sat down at the end of the table asked.

Betina responded. “Quite well, better than when we were married. We find divorce works fine for us. We almost never fight anymore.”

Heath smiled at the brunette, agreeing with his ex. “It’s so much simpler being friends. The boys seem fine splitting time with us.”

“Isn’t the twentieth century interesting?” the woman said, making more of a statement than asking a question. “I hope I could be so modern and accommodating. Sorry we haven’t been introduced. My name is Marjorie.”

The couple nodded to the newcomer at the table, and introduced themselves to the lady. She made a quick wave and placed some green beans into her mouth, temporarily cutting off her conversation.

After swallowing, Marjorie said, “I haven’t seen you two at a meeting before. Are you new members?”

Heath responded, “Betina has been a member and invited me. It’s my first meeting.”

Two speakers made presentations, and then donations were collected. As everyone stood to put on their jackets, Marjorie said to Heath, "How would you like to get a cup of coffee with me?"

Totally surprised by the invitation, the newest Sierra Club member took a closer look at the woman who made the offer. Unlike the flapper style, she had long brown hair. Her dark brown eyes highlighted a pretty face with a small "button" nose. Red lipstick was the only makeup he noticed. She wore a long black skirt and sensible flat-heeled winter leather boots. She pulled on a plain gray wool coat over a white blazer. Silver hoop earrings completed her conservative, almost late nineteenth century appearance. She seemed a total contrast to Kathryn's modern movie star style.

Heath smiled at the woman. "One second." He said, holding up a finger. He turned to his ex-wife and said, "Do you mind me going off? I'd be happy to pay for your taxi."

Betina smiled, "I've got it covered. Have a good time, but for gosh sake, show a little restraint. No running off to Mexico. Okay?"

"I'll try and be careful." He turned back to Marjorie. "Do you really want coffee, or something a little stronger?"

"I'm a big girl, a drink would be nice."

"I know a place just down the hill on Geary." He presented his arm like a gentleman. The woman placed her hand at his elbow, touching him for the first time. No sparks or fireworks went off, but a wick was lit in a candle that would burn for a lifetime. The two walked out of the great Fairmont's lobby to busy Powell Street and down the hill as cable cars clanged past.

"Why did you invite me?" he asked.

"I hope you don't think I was too forward. I just like the fact that you get along with your ex. It shows character. Tell me about yourself. Have you always lived in San Francisco?"

"I grew up in Alameda, lived in the Bay Area all my life. How about you? I think I hear an English accent?"

"I grew up in a little town Chalbridge, near Oxford. Father is a doctor and when I was fifteen we moved to Peru. He got a job with an oil company."

"Interesting, so you must comprende Español?"

"Sí, señor, y tú?"

"No, no, but I just came back from Mexico so I got used to hearing it for a week."

"On business?"

"Well it's a long story. Maybe I'll tell you about my trip sometime."

"Why not now?"

They entered the speakeasy. The bouncer knew Heath and opened the door that lead to a staircase into the illicit bar. "What are you drinking?" Heath asked.

"What's good here?"

"How about an Irish coffee?"

"Really? An Irish coffee for an English woman?" she said with a laugh. "Actually that would be fine."

He turned to the bartender, "One Irish coffee and a Canadian whiskey please. Marjorie, I think I better get to know you a little better before I tell you my Mexico story."

"That good?"

He changed the subject, "So why did you come to San Francisco?"

"My father's contract was ending and my family was moving back to England. I always wanted to visit the States and reckoned it was now or never. I caught a steamer from Lima to San Francisco."

"So are you living here permanently?"

"I don't know. I'm here on a work visa, but I fell in love with San Francisco the second I sailed through the Golden Gate. It's all so new, not like old England, and the hills kind of remind me of Peru."

"Well it is new, rebuilt since the earthquake."

"Were you here?"

"Of course." He looked past her for a moment, back in time, and then took a long drink of his whiskey, bringing him back to the dark bar.

"Was it quite awful?"

"It was devastating. The whole city either fell from the quake or burned from the fire that followed."

Marjorie put a hand on his arm, lending support. "You were alright, and your family?"

"Yes, we were lucky."

She finished her drink and said, "It's getting late and I have to go, but I'd like to see you again."

"Do you want me to accompany you home?"

"I live kind of far away. I have a room in a house on Clement out towards the ocean. I take the Geary streetcar."

"Come on, it's late for a woman to ride the trolley home. I'll get us a cab."

They walked back to Powell. The wind had picked up and the air smelled damp, rain was coming. Heath hailed a taxi and they boarded just as the sky opened up and large raindrops attacked the car's windows.

"Thank you, Mr. Angelo; it seems you've saved me from a soaking on the way home." She smiled and touched his hand. Heath thought her English accent sounded classy, and moved his hand under hers, keeping the connection.

"I would like to see you again also, but I've just ended a whirlwind love affair, so I'd like to take things slowly."

The cold rain blasted the car and Marjorie felt like snuggling with the warm man next to her. It had been awhile since she had been on a date and she felt a strong yearning inside of her. A cattle baron in Peru broke her heart. That was one of the reasons she came to California to get a new start.

"Slow would be fine," she said.

"Are you free Friday night?"

"If you don't mind meeting me after work. I'll get off at seven, so I'll be downtown."

"Where should I pick you up?"

"I work at Macy's, the perfume counter."

"Works for me."

The traffic was light and they pulled up to her house. He held an umbrella for her and he waited for the lady to unlock her door. Heath held out his hand to shake goodnight. She took it, but leaned forward to kiss him on the cheek. "Goodnight Heath".

"Goodnight Marjorie," and he fled back to the cab.

The young Englishwoman walked into the house and found her roommate Joanne awake on the couch reading.

"Did you have a good night?" Joanne asked.

"Very good." She smiled but wrinkled her brow. "I think I just met the man with whom I'm going to spend the rest of my life."

DECEMBER 31, 1924

The countdown started, ten seconds until midnight and the New Year. Heath and Marjorie were back at the Fairmont. The room at the top with the unmatched view of the city they loved, he the native, she the immigrant. Each had a funny pointed hat on their head. The jazz band stood quiet and waited watching the clock with all in the room.

The couple turned away from the view and the lights below to face each other, gazing into his blue and her brown eyes. "Ten, nine, eight, seven, six, five, four, three, two, one, zero. Happy New Year!" the band yelled into the microphone.

From Chinatown, they could hear the explosions of fireworks. The music started to play and Heath took the lady from England in his arms and they kissed for the first time. Her lips tasted like mellow red wine. He kissed her again, lingering, tenderly. Tears welled up in her eyes.

"Why are you crying?" he asked.

"I'm happy".

They had spent the last two months getting to know each other. They explored the Bay Area together, and explored each other's souls. They talked of everything: the earthquake, Betina, Kathryn, England, Peru, her first love, his children, religion, philosophy, parents. He told her things he had not even shared with his first wife.

"I have a present for you." Marjorie told him. She produced a small box wrapped in a ribbon.

"Unfair, I didn't get you anything."

"I know and I didn't get you anything for Christmas. I want you to have this. Open it."

He pulled on the ribbon and opened the box. He found a small gold nugget with a vein of quartz crystal running through it.

"Wow!" He held it up and even in the dim light it sparkled.

"Before I left Peru I went to Machu Picchu. In the Indian village, I was taken to a medicine man whose ancestry went back to the ancient Incas. He sold me this stone. The elder put his hand on my head and told me to give this to a man and you will be bonded together like the quartz is bonded to the gold."

She leaned forward and kissed him, tasting his lips. He tasted bittersweet like dark chocolate.

"This is too much…I haven't asked….we haven't…."

"You will." She said confidently. "How can you escape three thousand years of Inca knowledge and a stone from the great Andes Mountains? The earth now links you to me."

Heath laughed loudly. He had been fighting his feelings. This was just too fast after his divorce with

Betina and his whirlwind romance with Kathryn, yet he realized he felt something with Marjorie he did not feel with either of those other two women; comfortable, at ease. He took her delicate hand in his and kissed its back, like an English gentleman he had seen in the movies.

FEBRUARY 14, 1925

Sea lions sunned themselves on the rocks. The huge males push the smaller ones back into the bay like boys playing king of the mountain. The winners of the game would bark loudly, lording over the enclave. Heath squinted as the sunlight glistened off the choppy water. Marjorie took his hand softly in hers, caressing his fingers. They both wore pants, not just as a symbol of their equality in their relationship but because of their activities of the day.

After taking the ferry from the city to Sausalito and having breakfast at a cute dive of a restaurant, they moved out to the trails north of town along the Marin coastline. Yellow mustard and blue lupin bloomed above the green grasses. The day was crisp but clear, tucked in between winter storms. The two attacked the hills, climbing to a peak covered by tall redwoods. Looking south, they could see across the bay to Alcatraz where convicts could share the view in this exceptionally clear day. Angel Island stood next to the prison rock, where Marjorie cleared customs to arrive on American shore. Behind was San Francisco where the Fairmont Hotel stood above the skyline of Knob Hill, announcing that the city was back from the shake of its foundation, born anew from the ashes.

Heath was back as well, reborn from his fiery rebound romance, ready to take on the rest of his life.

He had let Marjorie be the aggressor, romancing him rather than wooing her like a normal courtship in the early twentieth century. The roundtrip ten-mile hike was completed and Marjorie felt tired but fantastic, invigorated by the physical exertion.

Heath said, "I have a special Valentines present for you."

The Englishwoman smiled. "You remembered. Didn't…" She stopped in mid-sentence as the man got down on one knee and produced a small box, tied up with the same red ribbon that had enclosed her New Year's gift to him.

"Will you marry me?"

She smiled, playing with him, and put a finger under her chin like she was thinking. Finally she said, "You bloody well know I will marry you. The third time's a charm." Giggling she threw her arms around her man and kissed him all over his face, finally finding his mouth for a passionate yet tender embrace of his lips.

"Open it," he said, looking at her through squinted eyes from the glare off the water behind her. She tore at the ribbon and cracked open the box. A gold ring appeared. Marjorie held it up to the light to see that the gold ring was speckled with quartz crystal. Heath held up his nugget.

"Now you have a match."

"God, it's beautiful. Where did you find it?"

"You're not going to believe it. I found it in a pawn shop on Market Street. The owner told me that it had belonged to a woman who came to California on a wagon train. It was given to her by her husband in Sonora during the Gold Rush."

Marjorie slipped it on her finger. It was a perfect fit, like it had been made for her.

The ferry pulled in from San Francisco and the passengers disembarked on the dock. The two lovers boarded the boat with many other Valentine couples returning to the city.

"I love Marin," Marjorie said with her arms out spinning on the bow like a little schoolgirl. "And I love you Mr. Angelo." She had never said it to him before, although she had thought it from the first day they met.

"I love you too, my darling Marjorie." He said, surrendering his Declaration of Independence to the British woman who had captured his heart.

JUNE 10, 1926

Alfred was dead. He was part of the generation that had seen a great change in American life. During his lifetime the United States had become a modern nation, a great world power. The automobile and electric light changed the fundamental way of life and large urban factories changed the way of doing business. The relatively small business of the Angelo and Son Box Company was expanding and prospering under Heath's leadership.

As God takes life, so God gives life. Two weeks after the funeral, Marjorie gave birth to a son, Alden, named after both a combination of both boys' grandfathers. With the prospect of being new parents, Marjorie and Heath decided to change lifestyles and move out of the city to raise their child. They bought a house and a plot of land at the base of Mount Tamalpais in Marin at the outer edge of a small town, Mill Valley.

Yellow mustard grew below the grapevines on the hills below the redwood trees of the mountain. The Angelo acreage also bloomed with apple blossoms. Marjorie, in touch with her English roots, was happy to be a landed lady in her newly adopted homeland. Her "manor house" was a simple place, a nineteenth century Victorian, but it was home, large enough to raise a family, not like the city apartment in which they had lived.

"Are you going to San Francisco to work today?" The new mother asked her husband.

"Yes, we have a shipment of boxes to get out. It would be fun if you could come. We could have lunch at that place next to the ferry building."

"Oh no, there's no way I'm going to travel with the new baby. I'll just stay here and be the milk cow," she said with a laugh. "But hurry back tonight. I have some steaks to cook on the barbeque. Look at me turning into a real American."

"It's a date sweetheart."

MAY 31, 1930

Four months earlier Mary was born to a family that loved her. Her older brother looked down at the baby in the crib and crunched his face.

"She smells funny." Alden said.

His mother said, "You smelled funny when your diapers were full. Can you get me that cloth over there?"

He watched as she folded the cotton square into a triangle and wrapped the just cleaned little girl into the diaper and fastened it with a safety pin. "I don't need no nappies no more!" the four year old said proudly. "I'm a big boy!"

"Yes, you have your own knickers now." She preferred the English word, rather than the American, "underpants."

Alden or Mary could not know that the stock market had crashed or that their neighbor's house would be for sale by January. That young couple had lost all their savings; the man his job, and could not pay their mortgage.

The Angelos were lucky. Of course Heath lost money when the stocks bottomed out, but his company and house were paid for with no mortgage. He had to lay off workers to tighten his business' belt but opportunity was there for people that survived. They would buy the foreclosed property next door at a bargain price.

Penny, the family dog, a two-year-old German Shepard, started barking loudly at the front door. A knock followed and with Heath working in the city, Marjorie apprehensively opened the front door to find a young man in his twenties standing hat in hand. His white cotton shirt was frayed and his expensive wool suit jacket was dirty and wrinkled.

"Excuse me, ma'am, but if you have any chores, I'll work for food." The dog sniffed at the man and stood guard inside thc doorframe.

"It's ok, Penny." The woman of the house said calmly. Alden hung at Marjorie's leg as she thought for a second and said, "There's some wood out back to chop. I'm busy in the kitchen. What's your Christian name, young man?"

"Laurence, err, Larry Adams, ma'am."

She fetched him the axe and pointed to the pile of wood to be chopped. Marjorie then went to the kitchen and cut a large piece of bread from the loaf she had just baked, found a hunk of goat cheese and an apple, putting them in a small paper bag. When he finished, Marjorie brought the package out to the hungry drifter who had lost his job as a clerk at Macy's in San Francisco, coincidentally, the very store she had worked at when she met Heath. He was the first of many drifters, laborers from San Francisco who would loose their jobs, and wander the countryside looking for work.

"Where are you headed now?" she asked.

"North. To Seattle to live with my sister and her husband. I'm hoping to find work there in a lumber camp."

She gave him the food and a quarter. "Good luck, Larry. I hope you find work in Seattle."

"Thank you so much," and he turned and walked back down the dirt driveway in his expensive black Oxfords that desperately needed a shine.

Mary and Alden had a warm home, bills paid, electric lights, heat during the winter rains, and shade trees to sit under in the summer sunshine. As the nation and the world descended into an economic and social abyss, the Angelos survived, and even prospered.

JUNE 12, 1931

"I fecl like Gulliver in the land of giants." Marjorie said as she stared up at the giant Redwoods that seemed to reach up endlessly towards the gaps in the blue sky above their highest green needles. The California Western Railroad and Navigation Company steam train chugged its way along the forested hillsides, counting six cars in total; five empty lumber cars and one passenger. The train was winding its way along the tracks of the Noyo River canyon toward the coast and the small town of Fort Bragg. The Angelo family was combining a holiday with business, looking for a cheaper lumber supply for the box company. The two teens, Heath Jr. and Ulysses, sat next to little Alden, playing with their younger half brother. Mom and dad were across the aisle with little Mary sitting up in her baby carriage, her teddy bear cuddled in her arms.

Marjorie felt alive in the Northern California woods. The grandeur overwhelmed her senses. She also loved being a mother, the woman always liked being around children. Having her own to nurture seemed as natural as the mother mallard and her ducklings swimming in the river below. Marjorie smiled as she saw the water birds out the big window as the train hopped around the next curve.

Mrs. Angelo pointed and said, "Look Mary, a mommy and baby ducks. Can you say 'duck'?"

The young girl was just starting to speak. She tried to say "duck" but it came out "dook." As they came around the next bend, the whole north side of the tracks showed miles of exposed clear cutting. All that was left were stumps and the slash of limbs left behind, too small to make lumber.

"Oh my God!" The woman cried as she viewed the carnage. "I know we need lumber, but isn't there a better way? This is awful." She said to her husband.

The exposed deforestation went on for miles along the tracks. Slashed stumps and stubble was all that was left of beautiful woods, leaving the hills exposed and naked. Her mood quickly changed to one of sadness. The majestic grandeur of the redwood forest was lost. She wondered if any trees would be left for her children.

The family returned to Highway 101, took the old Model T and explored further north. The Depression had hit the Mendocino economy and land values hard. For sale signs were almost as prominent as the tall Redwood trees they were nailed upon.

The Angelos found an old homestead for sale in forested land near Branscomb along Wilderness Road on the south fork of the Eel River. Marjorie was already in love with the property that called from an earlier era, before settlers displaced Native Americans and cut down the great forests of North America. The old homestead cabin was falling down. The farm meadow and fruit trees were in danger of being reclaimed by the native growth of the North Coast forest.

Heath looked up to see a Golden Eagle soaring above, scouting the meadow and the creek bed for prey. Hairs stood up on the back of his head and he was overcome by an almost religious experience.

"Marjorie, this could be our land."

She was so overwhelmed that fear came to her eyes. "Really? All this land? How could we possibly afford this?"

"The price of land has dropped so low that we could borrow on the company. This would be a great investment."

"Would we need to cut down these magnificent trees?"

"Let's see. I hope not."

The family headed back to Marin and San Francisco, but they had seen their future. Within months, the Angelo estate would include this majestic Mendocino forest.

March 24, 1933

It was late in the year for such a strong storm. Rain pelted down sideways, blown by the strong southern wind. Seven-year-old Alden felt a chill down his spine as he walked home from school. When he left that morning the sun was shining, the days were getting longer and spring was blooming. Honeybees flew by the boy on their way to grape and apple blossoms. His long sleeve white cotton shirt and slacks that his mom had laid out for him seemed quite warm enough for the early April day. But by noon, signs of an impending storm were showing. Puffy cumulous clouds started to appear. The winds started building, slowly at first, a gentle breeze, and then a steady south wind blew dust in a swirl on the playground. Alden could see the sky starting to sprinkle outside his classroom window. By the time the school bell rang, the storm attacked in earnest. Marjorie felt guilty. Heath had taken the truck to the ferry and was in San Francisco completing his duties at the box and basket company. Marjorie couldn't get the stupid old Model T started, so Alden would have to walk the half-mile from the bus stop to the house in the pouring rain. It couldn't be helped; besides, little Mary was being a pest. The young girl wouldn't go down for her nap and was causing trouble all afternoon.

When Alden walked in the front door, his mom greeted him with a quick kiss then told him "Get out of those wet clothes; I laid out a dry outfit on your bed."

Heath walked in the door an hour later, also soaking wet. He kissed his wife, then his petulant daughter, and went to change, dripping all the way to the bathroom. He heard his son cough as he undressed and got into a hot bath, which warmed him to his bones and cleaned the layer of dirt off his dermis. Marjorie came into the steamy bathroom, bringing her husband a glass of wine with a quick kiss.

"How did it go in the city?" she asked.

"Good. Despite the downfall, orders for boxes seemed to remain steady. The farmers on the coast and the central valley still need boxes for produce and with less of a workforce; I've been able to lower prices. How was your day?"

"I couldn't get the Ford started, even with the new electronic ignition you installed. Maybe it needs a tune-up."

"I'm afraid it may be showing its age, but it's a great car on the old dirt roads up in Mendocino, I hate to get rid of it. "

Alden coughed again and sneezed.

"I hope the boy doesn't get a cold. He walked home in the downpour." The mother said.

By evening Alden was complaining of a sore throat. His cheeks felt warm so Marjorie took out the glass mercury thermometer and after coating it with Vaseline, inserted it anally into the boy's rectum. Three minutes later, she held it up to the light. The liquid metal showed "100.5." The woman gave her son a child's flavored Bayer aspirin and tucked him in bed.

"He'll probably be better by morning." Heath calmly told his wife, and kissed her on the cheek. He then went to Alden's bed, kissed him on the forehead and said, "Sweet dreams, son. I hope you feel better."

"Goodnight, Dad."

Just after midnight Marjorie awoke with a mother's instinct that something was seriously wrong. Going to the boy's room, she arrived to see Alden violently vomiting to the side of his bed. He complained of hot and cold sweats. The thermometer now measured 102. She got the lethargic boy out of bed and into a cool bath to lower his body temperature. Heath was now awake and at his wife's side. "Honey, I think we should call Dr. Franks." He went to the kitchen and cranked the party line telephone hanging on the wall.

"What number please?"

"Operator, get me Dr. Franks please."

The phone rang at the doctor's home. Eight rings later he heard a sleepy voice. "This is Dr. Franks."

"This is Heath Angelo, sorry to bother you in the middle of the night, but Alden is very sick."

After relating the symptoms to the doctor, Mr. Angelo heard him say "Let me grab my bag, I'll be there within an hour, and continue what you are doing."

When the doctor arrived, he did a full examination, pulled medicine out of his bag, and said "Give him a teaspoon of this every four hours. If his temperature doesn't come down, call me in the morning."

By Sunday, Alden was in the hospital with pneumonia, wheezing under an oxygen mask. His parents were staying continually at the boy's side with little sleep. Betina came up from San Francisco to stay with Mary.

Bacteria grew by the thousands in the boy's lungs, as the sulfur medicine could not kill them fast enough. Mucus filled his alveoli and breathing became more and more difficult. His parents looked on with horror and helplessness. By evening the young boy's body started shutting down and he died that night. The couple's loss was overwhelming and they would carry the guilt and burden all their lives.

April 10, 1933

Marjorie heard his ghost again, coming from the empty bedroom. The boy's absence haunted her and she knew the sound was not just her imagination. There was a distant tapping sound coming from the second floor.

"Heath, you heard that, didn't you?"

"Actually I did. I'll go up and check it out."

As his wife sat knitting, Mary was playing on the floor with her dolly. The father crept carefully up the stairs and as quietly as possible opened the door to Alden's former bedroom. It stood empty, devoid of life, like an exhibit in a history museum. Clothing still hung in the closet and the boy's underwear was still folded neatly in the dresser. The man examined each corner, and then looked under the bed. 'Were they both hearing things?' he wondered. The man closed the door and sadly walked back down the steps, but before he completed the landing, he heard it again, the tapping. He turned and ran back up to the room. The window was closed, allowing no gap for a wind to blow in and cause the blinds to bang. What was that tapping sound? Was he going crazy, or was the room really haunted? Heath again descended, sitting down in the living room, only to hear tapping again. One look at her whitened face and he could tell Marjorie heard it also. Even Mary stopped her playing to look up.

Heath walked outside and looked up at the front room window. The answer to the question of the tapping noise was quickly apparent. A crow had seen his reflection in the evening glare on the windowpane, and like a canary pecking at a mirror in a cage; the large back bird was attacking his reflected image. Heath thought of the fictional raven from Edgar Allan Poe, the author of many a morbid ghost story. He asked himself was the crow sending him some kind of karmic signal. He told his wife about the bird and she shivered.

"This house is too big and too haunted."

The couple's depression matched the country's economic condition. Real estate and home values had plummeted with one important exception, Marin County, California. After years of planning, funding problems, and political infighting, the Golden Gate Bridge was under construction. This caused a great land speculation in the North Bay Arca County. Heath agreed with his wife, "I think it's time to sell this house and move to the Mendocino land. If we sell the business, we could pay off the homestead, rebuild the place, and get a clean start."

By August Angelo and Son Basket and Box Company was sold. The Marin property was disposed of, fetching a large profit. The family packed and overloaded their new truck with all their belongings to try their famc and fortune in a new land, like the pioneers coming to California almost a hundred years earlier.

JUNE 10, 1939

The fog turned back, retreating toward the cold waters of the Pacific as the summer sun rose over the majestically tall coastal mountain conifers. In the river, an otter played with her catch, a lamprey eel. This snake-like ancient fish whose relatives were on earth before the dinosaurs, gave the Eel River its name. Otters love to play with their food and this young female tossed the spineless fish into the air watching it flip above the bank frolicking like a Labrador retriever with a tennis ball. Her mate swam up and the aquatic mammal took his turn with the eel toss. The two lovers played with their food before they finally settled in to share the meaty meal.

Nine-year-old Mary Angelo watched from the opposite bank. The young girl grew up with her own personal live Discovery Channel. She had a view when the red-tail hawk swooped down and attacked a squirrel that dabbled too long looking for nuts. She had seen the big brown bears picking native blackberries along the vines that grew next to the dirt road. The girl heard the feral pigs roosting in the Manzanita. As she walked by, the pigs would cause the quail to flutter and take flight. She never saw a cougar but she came across a deer with her neck ripped out, a former feast of the mountain lion. Raccoons, ring-tailed cats and white-tailed does became her viewing companions, but she would never leave the cabin without her best friend, Ralph, the extraordinary German Sheppard. The girl's companion was the son of Penny, the family's older dog. Mary and the canine would wander the woods together. The dog was born in the forest and it was his home. He never chased the deer or other prey despite his genetic link to the carnivore wolf. The Angelo family was his pack and he acted like his human family. Curious and coexistent with any animals that were peaceful, but if any beast posed a threat to Mary, like a mama bear, Ralph would protect the girl with his life.

Summer was a magical time for Mary. After doing her chores, the girl felt free to explore. Girl and dog left the riverbank and walked up the road. The big dog stopped and barked a warning. Mary halted in her tracks, as she had learned to obey the dog's instincts. Looking up the rocky road, she saw the rattlesnake curled and ready to strike. Mary knew the snake was being defensive and called calmly to her dog.

"Come here, boy."

The dog retreated to the girl and they walked carefully around the reptile, allowing the animal to go back to sunning himself in the opening of the road.

The symbiosis of girl and dog allowed Heath and Marjorie to have confidence that the girl was safe on her short adventures. They had taught their daughter lessons to be at home in the forest that was their domain.

Ralph and Mary came up the road towards the homestead. Heath was thinning apples from the over laden fruit trees in the meadow. The family grew fruit and vegetables for home and for local market. The girl ran up to her father, excited to see him in the small orchard. She threw her arms around the sweaty man.

"Dad, you wouldn't believe what I saw today."

JANUARY 10, 1944

The Western Union man pulled up to the Angelo home after traveling the long drive in a steady rain from his office in Willits. He parked his company car, a grey 1941 Chevrolet. That was the last year passenger cars were built before the factories converted to war materials. The forty-five year old driver, Sean O'Brien, was age-exempt from the draft. The man walked up to the house and noticed the Silver Star in the window. He knew each star decal meant this house had a son in the military and that his sealed telegram probably brought bad news.

Sean knocked. When Marjorie opened the door to see a man dressed in a Western Union uniform, her knees buckled. 'Please, God, no.' she thought.

"Ma'am, are you Mrs. Angelo?"

"I am."

"I have a telegram for your husband," and he handed her the envelope.

Heath came up from behind. He had been working in the kitchen, fixing a leaky sink. The woman gave her husband the notice without opening the envelope. Mr. O'Brien waited at the door. The main part of his income came on tips, but he had delivered too many of these notices from the Armed Forces and did not want to be compensated by a family that had received horrific news.

Heath gave a look to Sean, trying to kill the messenger with his eyes. He attacked the envelope like he wanted to do it damage and pulled out the tele-typed page.

"This is to inform you that Private First Class Ulysses Angelo, is missing in action in the Philippines."

"Is that all?" Heath asked the Western Union man, passing the note to Marjorie.

"Yes sir."

In spite of his dread, Heath tipped the man at the door, then turned to his wife and said, "Betina must have gotten the same telegram. I'm going to Branscomb to the pay phone to call her."

"Do you want me to come with you?"

"No. Stay with Mary. I should be back soon."

Ulysses was missing, but alive when his parents received the telegram. The soldier had gone ashore with his unit on the island of Luzan in early December, well after McArthur's famous walk on the beach for his “I will return” photo shoot. Angelo’s platoon was part of the massive build up of army forces fighting to reclaim the Philippines from the stubborn Japanese occupation forces.

His squad moved up to the front and quickly encountered a well-entrenched machine gun nest. Lieutenant Franklin commanded as they took cover behind trees, “Corporal Diamond, you take Angelo and work your way to the right flank of that machine gun. We’ll give you cover and fire in exactly five minutes.”

“Will do, sir.” The corporal said and pointed to Ulysses to follow him.

It was the twenty-four year old private’s first action. Drafted back in forty-three, he had worked in a supply depot before being assigned to be part of the massive army invasion force in the Philippines.

The two American soldiers ducked into the woods and were ready to attack the flank of the Japanese gun. Suddenly, the enemy forces counter-attacked with a huge bonsai charge. Ulysses’ squad was overwhelmed and Corporal Diamond shouted to, “Follow me.”

The two ran deep into the jungle in full retreat, zigzagging as bullets flew around them. Out of breath, Ulysses stopped and looked up. He was alone! Corporal Diamond was nowhere in sight and he was surrounded by the enemy so there was no chance of yelling to find him.

The private decided to walk in the direction of their retreat, hoping to find the American frontlines. He had no compass and only a canteen for water and a day's k-rations for food. He had his rifle but his helmet had fallen off during his run. As he took personal inventory, he noticed that his dog tags were missing. Crouching behind a tree, the private listened carefully. He could hear Japanese to his left, so he tried to stay calm and walked deeper into the jungle forest. His days of hiking with his brother and father in the wilderness of California gave him some confidence in this otherwise desperate situation.

Lost and alone, Ulysses had no way of knowing he was going the wrong direction, moving further behind enemy lines. The sun went down, leaving Private Angelo hungry but not cold in the warm and humid climate of this Philippine island. He built a bed of leaves and despite his discomfort and fear, exhaustion overtook him and he slept.

In the morning, Private Angelo consumed half his food without trying to cook it, his need to avoid a fire, which could give away his position to the enemy. He hiked to the edge of the woods and spied a village, but a Japanese troop presence was obvious. The Private retreated back into the jungle.

He smashed coconuts with his rifle and collected other native fruit. Days turned into weeks. The California native hid, explored, and scavenged for food. His skin turned leathery and his uniform frayed in the rain and the sunshine.

DECEMBER 24, 1944

The American Army prepared a special Christmas Eve dinner for the troops. Big slices of ham, sweet potatoes, and green beans slopped over Private Dave Loab's mess kit and he ate quietly, between sips of grape juice. His squad was just off the front lines and the fighting had been ferocious, despite an overwhelming American advantage in air cover. The Japanese were tough, experienced, disciplined, and fanatic soldiers. The casualty rate in his squad was over fifty percent and he felt lucky to be alive. Loab was looking forward to the first piece of apple pie he will have eaten since he boarded the troop ship in San Francisco and headed for the Philippines. Dave was sitting on a big rock chewing when he looked down between his knees and saw a pair of dog tags almost buried under the dirt. He picked them up, noticing that the metal chain had been broken. "Ulysses Angelo" the name on the tags read. He turned them in to his Lieutenant, who sent the tags back to command.

The quarter master core processed the identification tags. Records showed that most of Private First Class Angelo's platoon-members had been identified as killed in action. Papers were issued and filed. Finally, the decision was made to notify the next of kin that Ulysses was missing in action.

JANUARY 1, 1945

Dawn awoke and so did Ulysses. He did not know it was New Year's Day 1945, the year the war would end and the atomic age was born. The missing soldier was jolted awake that morning by an extensive American artillery attack on the Japanese positions, with explosions close enough to feel the earth quake. Private Angelo advanced to the sounds of the guns knowing that a ground attack often follows artillery and the American army troops might be advancing in the village he scouted.

At the edge of the jungle, he climbed a tree to view a battle taking place before his eyes. Americans were advancing, firing at the resisting Japanese. Air core fighter planes flew close above him, strafing and bombing the enemy positions. Ulysses came out of the woods crawling on his belly towards a group of G.I.'s firing from behind rocks. The former lost soldier placed a clip in his carbine and joined the fight. Battlefields are confusing. Men fight together with their comrades but also alone. Another American on the firing line would barely be noticed in the heat of battle, yet to the other Americans, Ulysses looked like a refugee. His leggings were gone, helmet lost, clothing ripped and filthy.

Japanese forces counterattacked in a large wave but were met with overwhelming firepower. The

Asians fell like rain in a storm. Ulysses finally used his weapon and believed he shot two of the attacking enemy. His body was so pumped full of adrenaline that he could barely keep his arms from shaking as he shot. His training took over. Lying on his belly he fired, emptying his last clip.

"Cease fire!" Ulysses heard, his ears ringing and snot running down from his nose. The squad's sergeant, Ken Paulsen, looked over at the ragged new comer and asked, "What rock did you crawl out of?"

"Uh…I'm Private Angelo, um, Ulysses Angelo. I've been lost in the jungle."

"You look like crap, soldier." The sergeant raised his voice, "Carter, come here!"

"Yes, Sergeant."

"Take this lost puppy back to Lieutenant Gray and see what he wants to do with him."

Just like that, Ulysses Angelo returned to the U.S. Army. He was fed, issued a new helmet, and assigned as a replacement in Sergeant Paulsen's squad. No one reported him found to the quartermaster's core because no one in the field knew he had been reported missing. Ulysses joined his new squad and moved out towards Manila, engaging in extremely violent fighting. Supply filed papers for new dog tags. Still no one noticed that the soldier receiving them was reported missing in action. The military had a special nickname for this type of mistake: a “snafu”, situation normal, all fucked up.

Months later Heath received a letter from his missing son. Ulysses related his odyssey, heavily censored of course. Tears streamed down from the face of the father. His son was alive!

MAY 15, 1953

When the European settlers came to the North American shores, a blanket of trees covered the continent. A symbol of the American democracy is the young Abraham Lincoln chopping down trees, building a log cabin, and clearing land to farm. By the middle of the twentieth century, most of the land had been cleared. One of the continent's last forests covered the Pacific Northwest. In California, redwood trees had been harvested for a century but the fast growing second-growth was ready to be attacked. Douglas fir, once considered inferior lumber, was now as valuable as the gold that brought the forty-niners. As the post-war baby boom took off, the new families needed housing. With the new interstates, suburbia grew like weeds in a garden. The boxes of tract housing sprang up from Levittown, New York to Daly City, California. In the forest of Mendocino County, the sounds of the chainsaw drowned out the songs of the birds as the lumber companies invaded virgin land like the Nazi blitz in Europe ten years earlier.

Political realities had changed as well. The need for Franklin Roosevelt's social and conservation programs were gone. It was the time of the Cold War; the United States and capitalism versus the evil Soviet communists, with the very survival of the world at stake. Children practiced hiding under their desks, as pictures of atomic bomb blasts were depicted in the news reels, broadcast as public service announcements on the new televisions. The people of Mendocino County were prospering, working for the lumber companies, big and small. They couldn't understand why one family swam like salmon against the tide. "That Heath Angelo patrolling his property, protecting trees with a shot gun" was crazy, or worse, some kind of "commi pinko."

Money did grow on trees, but so did beauty. The forestland of Heath and Marjorie was a large natural island in the floodwaters of clear-cutting. The couple came to love the land like it was part of the family. Coming from England, Marjorie knew the importance of conservation. The forests of Britain were gone, long ago. Legendary Sherwood Forest of Robin Hood fame was down to a few hundred acres, where tourists came to see the trees of folklore, like the amusement park being built by Disney in southern California. So Heath came to protect his forest with a shotgun, like Robin Hood protected his with a bow.

The federal agency, Bureau of Land Management, owned much of the land that had joined the three thousand acres of the Angelo homestead. The government leased much of the BLM land to the California Pacific Lumber Company. Heath Sr. and Jr. stood over a table in the Angelo living room.

"They want to build a road right through the canyon and cut down the trees on the far bank of the Eel." Heath explained to his oldest son, now a lawyer with a considerable practice in San Francisco. The two poured over a large topographical map on the table.

"Dad, you know I've filed a writ in federal court to get an injunction to protect the land along the river. It's a long shot but there is precedent. National forest land along Yosemite and Yellowstone has been protected. I'm trying to show how clear-cutting erodes the land and how it has negative consequences to the river basin. Further, I'm trying to appeal to monetary interests. The cutting hurts other industries, like tourism and salmon fishing."

"When will the judge rule?"

"I expect to hear from the court within a week."

MAY 20, 1953

John McGregor working for Cal Pacific sat on a bulldozer along Wilderness Road. He was ready to start moving the land to start the logging road through the forest, along the Eel River, through the Angelo property. McGregor was a tough war veteran who drove a tank in Patton's army. He was making a good living plowing through the Mendocino countryside attacking the land the way he took on the Germans in France. Facing down the former Sherman tank driver's caterpillar tractor was Heath in his Ford pickup.

"Get that truck the hell out of the way or I'll ram you into the river."

"You're crossing my land, damn it, and if you get a dent in my truck, you and your company will be sued for more than you make in a year. Wanna chance it?"

"Listen Mr. Angelo, I've got my orders. I need to start this road."

"John, I'm not trying to get you in trouble or fired, but you're crossing my land. Go into town and call your boss and get a company rep here. They know about the lawsuit and need to recheck the map. You can't build this through my land!"

McGregor looked at Heath with his shotgun. The hedgerow country of Normandy had taught the former sergeant when it was prudent to retreat.

"I'll be back tomorrow."

"So will I."

Heath Jr. called with news that night. An injunction was issued with a cease and desist order to the lumber company.

MAY 21, 1953

John McGregor repeated his drive down Wilderness Road, parked his car and climbed back up on the bulldozer. As promised, Heath was there to meet him.

"Don't worry Mr. Angelo, I'm just here to remove the Cat."

The younger man started up the big tractor, put it in reverse and turned the vehicle around. John was secretly happy to remove the tank-like bulldozer. He looked around at the tall conifers and was glad to see them granted a stay of execution from the chainsaw blades. The veteran still believed in logging and was happy to have a good job, but there was lots more timber in the county. One place where nature was left on its own was ok with him.

As the sun reached its zenith, thermals rose above the riverbank. An osprey effortlessly rode the air currents, gliding overhead. Heath watched the white winged female stop and hover. The hawk dove and plucked a trout out of the clear Eel River water. This forest would continue to provide sanctuary. Mama bird brought the fish to her nest and fed the two hungry, waiting chicks, sustaining new life.

AUGUST 2, 1959

Mr. Angelo,

You must be a crazy son of a bitch.
Why would you stop the lumber company from cutting down the trees given to us by God?
It's scum like you that cost people their jobs.
God made people to rule over the Earth.
He made trees to be lumber, to be houses for the American people.
And remember, your house is made of wood and can burn.
And your trees can burn.
You and your Sierra Club friends remember that!
Get the hell out!

A concerned citizen

Marjorie read the letter delivered to the post office box in town. She added it to the pile of hate mail to be used as evidence if there were any serious attacks on the estate. Vandalism was common.

Marjorie asked her husband at the dinner table "Do you think you know who sent this one?"

"I have an idea, but it could be any number of the loggers or locals. I wouldn't even put it past the

California Pacific Lumber Company to have someone do it for them. Let's not fool ourselves, we have few friends and most of the local people work for the logging interests. They pay good wages and there aren't many other jobs up here. It's not easy swimming against the stream. Just ask the salmon trying to get up the Eel River after erosion from a clear cut had washed mud and gravel into the water."

"Sweetheart, you're preaching to the choir. What did you hear from Heath Jr. about that environmental organization?"

"Nature Conservancy, it looks real good. They will buy the land and turn it into a preserve. We can live on the estate for the rest of our lives and then one generation after us. The trees and the forest will be safe; we'll even have a little to live on, paying us $100,000 for all three thousand acres."

The Angelos were entering into the contract because government property taxes were based on the value of the land. The trees were assessed as timber, like a crop, whether the wood was harvested or left standing. It was a "catch-22" that favored the lumber companies and almost forced all land holders to cut down the forest. Nature Conservancy provided an alternative. This organization started earlier in the decade on the east coast, preserving endangered ecosystems. Funded by individual and corporate donations, this non-profit group was in position to help protect this unique California coastal range environment.

"Are we going to San Francisco to sign the paperwork?"

"No, actually they all want to come here for a signing ceremony."

"Well that will be exciting. Probably drive the locals crazy." The woman looked into her husband's eyes. "Heath, remember when we met at that Sierra Club Meeting?"

"Of course."

"Remember me saying I wanted to make a difference, helping the environment. I had no idea back then that we could do so much..." Tears welled up in the lady's eyes. "I'm so proud of you."

Heath kissed his wife on the cheek, tasting her tears. He said simply, "I love you."

JUNE 27, 1968

Marjorie and Heath sat on the porch. Two does and a fawn grazed in the meadow. The sunshine blazed down burning off the morning dew. A house had been built at the entrance of the Northern California Coast Range Preserve and a caretaker had taken up residency, handling all the preserve's business, yet the Angelo couple felt quite at home in the forest in their cabin. The young caretaker, Fred Lancing, asked the Angelos if it would be all right if new neighbors visited them. The retired couple said they were fine with the idea.

"No fog this morning. I'll bet it hits eighty five today," Heath said.

"Do you see that woodpecker? I've been listening to him all morning."

"Oh yeah, there he is on the old live oak."

Just then the hum of an air-cooled engine could be heard before a Volkswagen mini bus appeared coming down Wilderness Road. The vehicle was splashed in paint, many colors of the rainbow. A big round peace sign sticker covered the lower passenger side of the windshield. The automobile stopped on the road in front of the house and a young man and woman emerged.

"Hi." The young lady said, waving as she sauntered up to the deck, followed by her male companion. The woman had long brown, curly hair and was wearing a very short yellow floral mini dress, wide black belt, and multicolored beads around her neck. The young man sported very long straight blonde hair, cutoff jean shorts and a purple tie-dye t-shirt. They looked like what they were; refugees from the summer of love, moving north from the Haight-Ashbury district of San Francisco.

"I'm Sally and this is Jerry."

The four shook hands.

"Nice to meet you," the old man said, a look of amusement on his face. "I am Heath and this is Marjorie."

"Of course we know who you are." Jerry stated.

"Would you two like a drink?" Heath said, playing host.

"Sure, but we brought you something. Maybe you'd like to open this." Sally produced a bottle of Ripple wine.

Marjorie accepted the screw-top bottle and said, "How bout some bourbon?" She produced a bottle of George Dickle and as the young couple nodded she poured them each two fingers in a low-ball glass. "You might want to sip this."

"Where are you kids from?" Heath asked.

"Iowa, near Des Moines, left over a year ago and were in San Francisco. It was fun partying there, grooving to the music, but totally crazy, so sixteen of us pooled our money and invested in a place just down the road from you. You know, the old Eaton land. We wanted to get back to a natural place so we are starting a commune." Jerry said and produced a joint. "Want some?"

Marjorie's eyes got wide. "That's marijuana. That's stuff's supposed to be dangerous."

Jerry insisted, "No, it's harmless fun. I thought you might wanna try some."

"No thanks" the older couple said, almost at the same time.

Marjorie asked, "What's a commune?"

Jerry answered, "Well, we all have invested together; some more, some less, but we will farm democratically. We're even writing a constitution.

Sally said, "Everyone wants to meet you two. You're legends. Will you come to dinner?"

"We'd love to," Marjorie said, knowing she would have to prod Heath. "How old are you guys?"

"I'm twenty, and Sally is nineteen."

The young girl gushed, "We just love it up here and your place is amazing."

Marjorie noticed that below her short skirt, Sally's legs were unshaved. Her underarm hair was also evident. The first hippies had arrived. A population revolution was taking place in Mendocino. Within a couple of decades, the logging industry practices that were environmentally unstable would itself become an endangered species. A new economy would be built. The wine industry, tourism, and the agriculture of the illicit drug marijuana would become major occupations. The way the locals would view the Northern California Coast Range Preserve and the Angelo family would flip from one of disdain to one of reverence.

Sally asked, "Do you have children?"

"I have grandchildren." Heath replied.

"That's far out. We can't wait to have children in our commune." Jerry said.

"We have another present for you," and the young woman reached down and pulled a tin out of her bag. "Chocolate chip cookies, Jerry made them."

"Don't worry," the young man said. "I didn't cook any pot into this batch.

A smile came to Marjorie's face. "By coincidence I just made some cookies. You know one of the objectives of this preserve is scientific observation. I'll put one of the cookies that you made, Jerry, with a cookie that I made. That's one male and one female cookie. Let's see if we get any baby cookies.

Laughter ensued, and echoed in the trees.